Down with the Poor!

By Shumona Sinha

Translated from the French by
Teresa Lavender Fagan

DEEP VELLUM PUBLISHING

DALLAS, TEXAS

Deep Vellum Publishing
3000 Commerce St., Dallas, Texas 75226
deepvellum.org · @deepvellum

Deep Vellum is a 501c3 nonprofit literary arts organization
founded in 2013 with the mission to bring
the world into conversation through literature.

FIRST EDITION, 2023

LIBRARY OF CONGRESS CATALOGING-IN-PUBLICATION DATA

Names: Sinha, Shumona, 1973– author. | Fagan, Teresa Lavender, translator.
Title: Down with the poor! / by Shumona Sinha ; translated from the French
by Teresa Lavender Fagan.
Other titles: Assomons les pauvres! English
Description: First edition. | Dallas, Texas : Deep Vellum Publishing, 2023.
Identifiers: LCCN 2023006856 | ISBN 9781646052134 (trade paperback) | ISBN
9781646052394 (ebook)
Subjects: LCGFT: Novels.
Classification: LCC PQ3979.3.S54 A9413 2023 | DDC
843/.92—dc23/eng/20230405
LC record available at https://lccn.loc.gov/2023006856

ISBN (TPB) 978-1-64605-213-4 | ISBN (Ebook) 978-1-64605-239-4

Support for this publication has been provided in part by the Amazon Literary Partnership, National Endowment for the Arts, the Texas Commission on the Arts, the City of Dallas Office of Arts and Culture, and the George and Fay Young Foundation.

This work received support from the Cultural Services of the French Embassy in the United States through their publishing assistance program.

Cover design by Alban Fischer

Interior layout and typesetting by KGT

PRINTED IN THE UNITED STATES OF AMERICA

'For the ancient Greeks, the word for liberty (*eleutheria*) was defined as the possibility to move freely from place to place (*to elthein opou erâ*) . . . In the Greek verb *eleusomai* (to go wherever one wants) wild beasts come alive – as opposed to domesticated animals enclosed by fences, barbed-wire, barriers.'

Pascal Quignard, *La Barque silencieuse*

CONTENTS

White desire 1

Cherries in your mouth 4

On the other side of things 10

Kali's tongue 15

The man with a guava tree 19

Dealers of men 25

The land of clay 30

Zebra-striped life 39

I'm going to tell you the truth 49

Robin Hood 60

A giant hibiscus 63

The belly of the fish 69

My mother's hair 75

Chechen Eve 79

To love is to betray 82

The public swimming pool 88

The female knight and the mullahs 95

The wisteria woman 105

Impossible geometry 111

Narco-pirate 115

The night as confused as a blushing virgin 118

The lizard in the sand 125

White desire

Weary and defeated, I collapse onto the damp floor of
my cell and think about those people who swarmed
the seas like repellent jellyfish and heaved themselves
up onto foreign shores. They were interviewed in half-
hidden, half-open offices on the outskirts of the city. It
was my job, and that of many others, to interpret their
stories from one language to another, from the language
of the petitioner to that of the host country. Stories filled
with tears, bitter and cruel, winter stories, dirty rain and
muddy streets, stories of monsoons so interminable that
it seemed the sky would come crashing down.

I never imagined the path would be so short, that there
could be a path, a shortcut, between the interview rooms
and the damp cell in the police station where since yesterday I have been sketching my own family tree, the lines
of my thoughts and my wanderings, the combinations of
time and space, to justify my course and reconstruct the
scene; so people will understand my sudden urge to strike
the man, one of those immigrants, with a wine bottle. A
shiver runs up my spine. I'm afraid of myself. The woman
who grabbed the bottle without looking at it, raised it up,

felt its weight as she gripped it tighter so it wouldn't slip from her hand, then aimed at his head, black with hatred, mouth frothing with insults, and struck him.

A few months earlier, I had slammed the door in my boyfriend's face, as well as that of the office where I was working. It was a year of break-ups, of scarcity, of a lack of everything. I was living in a state of exasperation and confusion. The city seemed closed to me; its huge green, wooden openwork doors with metal doorknobs polished and darkened over time were heavy once again, no longer moving beneath my hand. Sometimes, my entire body pushing, I tried to open them as if I were attempting to bring up a sunken boat. It was agonizing to see closed doors in a city, in a country I loved, when I had put so much effort into opening them.

Then I had been hired to work as an interpreter and the language gymnastics began. There, all men looked alike. They had fled the land of clay swallowed by the black bay, their only viaticum the tale of migrating people. The weary slurring of their voices penetrated my summer days, slow and lazy, and everything blended together and was mixed in my head, which for a long time had been able to erase the memory of poverty. Their stories were like stories. No difference at all. Except for a few details, dates and names, accents and scars. It was as if a single Story were being told by hundreds of people, and the mythology had become the truth. A single tale and many crimes: rapes, murders, assaults, political and religious persecution. They were unfortunate *tusi-talas*, unwilling *tusi-talas*. I listened to their stories composed of choppy, cut-off, expectorated sentences. They memorized them and regurgitated them in front of the computer screen. Human rights do not mean the right to escape poverty. In any case, you didn't have the right to utter the word *poverty*. You needed a more noble reason, one that would justify political asylum. Neither poverty nor avenging nature that had devastated their land could justify their exile, their mad hope for survival. No law allowed them to enter here in this European country if they didn't have political, or even religious reasons, if they didn't demonstrate the serious consequences of persecution. So they had to hide, forget, unlearn the truth and invent another one: the tales of migrating peoples; with broken wings, filthy, stinking feathers; with dreams as sad as the rags on their backs.

A dream is a precocious memory. A dream is that desire which makes us travel miles, cross borders, seas and oceans; one that projects on the gray curtain of the brain the spatter of colors and the shades of another life. And people swarm the sea like repellent jellyfish and heave themselves up onto foreign shores.

Cherries in your mouth

The Earth kept turning as well as could be expected. Nature reshaped itself, more spectacularly in countries of the south than in those of the north. Rivers overflowed here and there. Lands drowned, with their rice fields and their dunes filled with coconut trees, with their thatch-roof huts, their mosques and their temples. And people kept climbing up to the safer, drier countries.

'What about you? Were you born here? Did you leave your country early? Are you mixed race?' asked the man leading the interrogation, the one I've been calling Monsieur K. ever since I arrived here at the police station, since his last name is long and filled with consonants and I can never remember it.

'What's *early* and what's *late*? I could spend my entire life here and never belong in this country.'

I immediately regretted saying those words, whose meanings were ambiguous. I should have quite simply stated the country where I was born, which corresponded to the color of my skin, the color of clay, which would always connect me to the man I attacked. And yet, I told myself, it wasn't particularly difficult to see the differences between him and me, to identify exactly the social classes we belonged to and to understand exactly how far apart we really were.

My mind wandering, I thought about the panda I had adopted a few months earlier, about the brown envelope with the black, cheerful logo; they assured me that they were receiving enough money for his bamboo shoots. I had friends who had gone at least once in their lives to clean beaches where birds were dying, smothered in oil. Engineers, teachers, volunteers with NGOs, exhausted by their daily commute for work, they became Buddhists. They always went to demonstrations where red flags poked up like vibrant poppies, and they opted for the luminous silence of monasteries when Hawking's theories became too obscure. And all the while, there were just as many people expelled.

Yesterday, I was taken to a room with windows and light wood partitions. It seemed identical to the semi-opaque, semi-transparent offices on the outskirts of the city where I worked. Then they took me to this underground room, without windows, in the underground parking lot of a seemingly labyrinthine building. Out of the shadows emerged Monsieur K., like a pale, fragile flame. He was to take my deposition. We were seated at a round table. The room felt padded. The rough concrete of the walls was inadequately softened by the dark blue carpet. Monsieur K. was smiling from the start. Apologized several times for the stark dinginess of the place.

His smile was pale and awkward. He was a nice fellow who might blush at the idea of tricking others. He was dancing around the matter at hand. What he wanted to know wasn't complicated. On the surface. But only on the surface. I muttered and stammered while explaining the reason I was here, in this country, why I had grabbed the bottle and smashed it on that guy's head. At the same time, I watched Monsieur K.'s strange modus operandi. He would advance with his questions, retreat, start again, he asked for justifications, tried to reconstruct events.

'So, out of love? Love of the language? Or you had dreamt of earning a living here?'

'Love of the language, I suppose… Turn it into a profession, it happened as it happened, over the years…'

'It wasn't a snap decision? Nothing random? Everything was calculated? You knew that you were going to settle in this country? Did you make the decision, or was it your family?'

I didn't know how to tell him, but I still tried to explain the culmination of a slow plan, nothing to do with family or professional obligations. I wanted to explain to him the hidden desire, the desire born of long hours spent with books. The fascination. The intoxication. The images of a life led through a foreign language. To swim and drown in it. And my rejection of all that fell short, of what couldn't enlighten, of what unfailingly plunged me into a spiritual morass.

'You mean to say that you're capable of hating those who haven't attained your intellectual level? Those who have remained at the foot of the ladder?'

I bit my tongue and wondered if that was true, if I was actually capable of hating, if latent hatred had suddenly bubbled up in me before violently erupting, then overflowed onto that man.

It was now my turn to be on the other side of a hidden computer screen on which Monsieur K. was taking down notes about my every word and gesture. This role reversal was humiliating. The way he looked at me, with an increasingly mocking smile, was mortifying. To save face, to present a respectable front, I started preparing my words the way you roll cherries around in your mouth before biting into them. I could see red drops squirting onto his blond face. It was a year of coincidences. I was changing roles, moving position, in front of and across from the computer, I formed a strange double figure like the ones in a shadow theater.

The Peugeots and the Mercedes were leaving, flaying the concrete surface of the parking lot. I rocked my chair, forward and backward and backward and forward. I crossed my left leg over my right leg, or maybe the other way round. I placed my hands on the table as if my fingerprints were being taken. I sensed that tectonic plates were moving over tectonic plates. People from the south who were traveling upwards bothered people from the north. The Earth was the sow who could no longer feed her excessive number of piglets. Wallowing in the mud, she groaned.

Monsieur K. brushed his lips with his thumb. He wasn't smiling anymore, even when I mentioned my latest flight. Awakened in the middle of the journey, I had seen through the window a land that looked vast and red hot like incandescent iron. Not a single trace of green or blue. Nature was playing a bad joke; had made an inept drawing. How did people live down there? There was nothing. Still dazzling under the sun, exhausted after a long day, that land looked like an open wound. The Soviet canons and tanks and soldiers had left this region of the Earth a long time ago. From the plane's window it was a bright red metaphor, indifferent and generous at the same time; a beauty from another time, from another era.

We paused on that image.

A few minutes earlier I had told him how, shortly after being hired at the office on the outskirts of the city, my life had taken a turn, with work, the RER commuter train, and evenings resigned to dull entertainment. Had told him how my life at that time resembled an art film from an emerging country, Asian, vaguely realistic, syncopated with semi-pornographic scenes – couplings in toilets and hallways as acts of rebellion. Minimal movements, like those of an ant, forearms raised, mute cries. But there was no longer anything to invent or to seek, all that was left was to change positions in toilet cubicles and believe you were liberated from social laws. To destroy any sort of dependency and feel free in that state of destruction, but it was just a new type of prison in which you went around in circles, thoughts churning. Thinking about the airplane window and the bright red earth did me good. Pulled me off the floor of the toilet stalls. Like levitating. Like taking off.

We remained on that threshold, between half-secrecy and half-transparency, between trust and suspicion. He was a sweet fellow who probably blushed at the idea of being suspicious of others. But that's the way he had been trained. With an invisible scalpel he wanted to dissect my thoughts. He told me he still didn't understand why I had attacked a poor immigrant seeking political asylum. But he was proceeding in a way that would enable him to reach the secret truth hidden deep inside me. It was no longer simply a matter of a random attack in a public place. He was expecting to reveal a twisted labyrinth of thoughts, a muddy spring of hatred, the rage that had suddenly surged causing a woman of color to attack a man of color, in an attempt to crush his skull.

On the other side of things

The offices where the raggedy petitioners came to plead their cases, dragging their feet, holding babies, but usually alone, were located in barren areas, beyond the city limits. Where the wind picked up. The wind picked up and died down and picked up again. Dust flew and spun around. The battlefield flared up. The sound of the RER, its corroded screeching, steel against steel, its criss-crossing rails stretching into the horizon, to even more barren zones, the sun bursting onto the tracks, factories rising up against the white sky. The veterans of the city, artists and activists, librarians, booksellers, teachers and protesters, were beginning to inhabit these hidden places. They felt proud to have discovered another face of their city, a more secret one, more subterranean, not as colorful, 'but swarming with life, where there's heart, and where there are *real people*', they said. It didn't matter that the country's leaders had obviously not fallen under the spell of these neighborhoods that were still under construction, or already abandoned. They had found them just right for building sad offices that received a throng of people who did not and who, most likely, never would belong here. The type of throng that could not, nor perhaps would not, blend into the glamorous whirl of the city's chic neighborhoods.

Emerging from the suburban train station, you turned left. Crossed the cracked asphalt street, avoiding the puddles and the gray and green public works fences. The street sloped downward. It turned in a semicircle and kept descending, you passed steps and flowerbeds. A guy with a beard had decided to settle down on a section of the steps. His German Shepherds were resting, their tongues hanging out. The man was scribbling on a bit of paper. Up close, you could see he was working on a sudoku puzzle in an old newspaper. Moldy green letters. Dirty, damp pages. The street continued under a bridge. Several streets merged into one. A palm with fingers spread out. RER trains passed above. Water dripped from the bare concrete overhang. Then overwhelming emptiness. To the left, an endless string of buildings, tall and ambitious, full of tension hidden behind the mirrored windows, standing together like a wall. Opposite, the wind picked up. The ring road swallowed streams of cars and spit them out beyond the city limits. The wind would play, becoming beyond wicked when you turned the corner of the wall of buildings. For a moment it seemed to have died down. It returned wilder than ever out of an unexpected empty and dizzying corridor between two buildings. The street turned left again. And you could already see the scattered lines of desperate people. They stood in groups reflecting their countries of origin. They were darker than their shadows at noon. Together they appeared as a huge, unforeseen cloud which at any moment could spread over the city. The wind finally died down around them.

A short distance away stood the door of the privileged. Of those who decide. Those who help decide – the language gymnasts, legal interpreters. Those who no longer have a shadow or a cloud over their face. Of various origins, they had wandered for a long time before arriving here, in their lucky country. Their lives crossed and blended like tangled paths, paths that descend to the dark knots of history. But the language gymnasts had achieved their goal. They had crossed the barbed-wire fences and the no-man's-land, the troubled waters, the stormy skies, the administrative desks; they had proven their merit, their legitimacy, they had fought and they had won. Their burden, their baggage, wasn't just in the hold of an airplane, but also on their shoulders. Invisible, heavy, dirty. Or in their bellies, like a post-term fetus, whose birth would be painful, bloody, most likely doomed. They hide it, cover it without knowing it and attempt to learn new social codes. But the codes of a new life bring knots of anxiety. Still in the belly, making you nauseous. If only we could vomit out all our ancient history.

Here, the interpreters from different continents and countries rub shoulders, yet it is but a false proximity, disorienting, divergent. Barbed-wire fences between us. A no-man's-land between us. Getting to know the other would be as perilous as crossing borders, seas, and oceans. Each person a world unto themselves. Each person holds an entire world within, a world in disorder. Beneath apparently common features, the citizens of the global village, all together and at the same time so alone, scatter into infinity. Sometimes we meet. The sons of corporate leaders and the sons of village imams, PhD students and sellers of vegetables, the Caucasian and the Russian women, the Albanian and the Armenian, the Indian and the Sinhalese, the Bengali and the Chakma, the Mongolian and the Nepalese, the Congolese and the Chadian, the Kurd and the Arab, Turks and Arabs, Arabs and Pakistanis, all wallowing in the same boredom, and each one awaits his or her turn before performing the language gymnastics. Here, the interpreters from mutating and ambitious countries, from orphan and resentful countries, all together have pinky-sworn not to become the *boot-lickers* of the countries in the north. Not to forget. To always light a candle on the secret altar of their memory. Memory is a religion. A war. Here, war is good. To knock down doors, destroy high walls, and be allowed in.

Every day, for months, I pressed the blue button. I pulled the door handle even before it was clicked open. I took out my ID card. Never a morning person, I pretended to smile. The guard playfully held out a daily pass. A moment later, the ID reader allowed me to pass onto the other side of things. The badge reader reads the laminated card and allows us to proceed onto the other side. Of the city limits. Of History. Lets us enter into the so-called privileged zones. Then begins the nightmarish chaos, the mixed blood of civilizations.

Kali's tongue

I awaken in the middle of the night and the anguish, like boiling oil in my skull, roils and sloshes whenever I move. I call to the policeman, who is dozing sitting up on a stool in front of the bars. In the restroom my head hangs close to the ground. The tips of my hair touch and sweep the dirty tiles from which there still emerge the faces and bodies of monsters, beasts, actors, shouters, criers, grimacing, complacent, puzzled, tormented people. They appear when I blink my eyes, disappear when I blink my eyes.

In my head I keep seeing the procession of people who enter the invisible places in this country. It was a year of transgressions, of semi-opaque offices. It was a year of tense triangles. Between him and me, between him and her, between her and me, between us: petitioner, officer, and translator. The one who pleaded, she who decided, and I who brought them together. Words poured out like rain. Question marks piled up on the blank screen even before questions had been asked. I saw men bite the dust of hope.

I did this work because I loved language gymnastics. I

spoke twice as much as anyone else. The officer spoke her language, the language of the host country, the language of glass-walled offices. The petitioner spoke his supplicant's language, the language of the hidden, the language of the ghetto. And I repeated what he said, translated it and served it up piping hot. The foreign language melted in my mouth, leaving its aroma. When I said the words, those of my native language, they turned awkwardly in my mouth, paralyzed my tongue, echoed in my head, hammered my brain like the wrong notes on a wobbly piano. It was a rope bridge, thin, quivering, between the petitioners and me. I had to lean toward each one of them to hold out my hand, lean into their dismembered, chopped-up sentences, fish for their disjointed words and reassemble them, weave them together to make them sound coherent. We spoke the same language, ours, but it was like shouting from my ninth-floor apartment to a passer-by on the street, to a beggar crouching and hidden in his dirty rags. Even worse, sometimes my words seemed to stun them, as if I had thrown boiling water at their heads. Sometimes they pulled themselves together and attacked us. When the questions began to make them uneasy, when they stammered and were ashamed of stammering, when they lied and knew they were lying, they grew insidiously angry and shouted that we didn't understand their language. They shouted that I wasn't translating what they said. They shrieked that I didn't understand their language, that it wasn't my language.

They had the right to criticize my work since no woman worthy of the name works. No village neighbor woman they recognized up close or far away stooped so low as to expose herself to the world, to allow herself to earn a living all alone, as if there were no more men on earth. And what's more, who dared to question them, the men! In the good old days, the days before all these journeys from sea to sea and from office to office, when the men who grew rice and sold spices went home without having to show thousands of papers, they would have knocked down a woman who spoke to them with her head high, her voice strong, who poked around in their secrets, claimed to challenge their erroneous, contradictory words. What was absurd was women questioning them and they, men, answering the women.

This was when I could have cracked a skull. When the lying, begrudging, sprawling words took hold of, wove around and smothered my brain. When that chaotic world invaded my body, my territory, and there wasn't a shred of peace left inside.

I wonder if Monsieur K. was right to seek the trail of hatred in me. When confronted with these insistent, miserable and unhealthy men, my heart was like a dog hunkering under a bridge when it rains. I tried to escape, to no longer exist, not to utter another word, I no longer wanted to have to raise my eyes to those faces crying out their woes, frothing with threats and insults. To erect a high wall between that endless procession of men and me. Diminished men, dwarfed, crushed by fear, or perhaps by hope, reduced to case or file numbers, men who had paid too dearly for their desire for a white horizon, for their European dream. Stunted, deformed, half-blind men, piled on top of each other in basements; they sprouted during the night, taking root in a land they didn't like but which they desired. In the end, it was like a casual fling between those men and this country; it was lust without love. At dawn the men came out of the dark caves in which the suffocating smell of spices and incense mixed with that of urine and sweat, and filled our offices. For a few minutes or a few hours, the mist of a distant land floated near the ceiling. It recalled the slow clouds swollen with rain, lolling like cows, coconut and mango trees swaying, sweeping the dark surface of the sky, the impatient rivers and the fish that left their clay nests and moved in a frenzy on the surface of the water, their mouths round and gaping. As soon as they entered, these men exuded the back rooms of the falsely chic shops and restaurants of the city. They reminded me of filth, the dirty water and the depressing clatter of cheap dishes, the bitter scent of exotic fabrics. They were the reverse side of the embroidery, they were the black backs of over-used pans, they were the hidden faces at a masquerade. The officers questioned them, they responded, I translated, I was the link.

The man with a guava tree

His eyes were round and he seemed permanently stunned. I remember that several times I had to ask him if he understood what I was saying. I thought he might be simple-minded. He always took a few seconds before opening his mouth, to swallow his saliva like a fish in need of air, only then did he say a few words. Hesitant. Inaudible. Terrified. I then knew that in his head there was a thin wire of a tale upon which he was balancing, advancing with trembling legs. A trapeze artist he was not. Rather a bungling village idiot the traveling circus had found amusing enough to put in their show. He was forced to get up on the high wire.

'We hunt down those who cross the border. But what about those who bring them, make them work off the books, those who set up this slave machine?' said the frustrated officer, a glorious forty-something woman. Her hair was cut short, golden brown; from time to time she pushed it back with a nimble hand, looking excited and tense like a cat watching a really stupid mouse.

'Slaves?'

I was polite but I could scarcely hide my joy, believing I was on the verge of discovering one of life's great truths.

'Exactly! They're brought here to work. And who do you think lines their own pockets? That's right! By making them pay for their passport, the journey, and the story.'

'You mean they also buy their stories?!'

She shrugged her shoulders. And raised her eyebrows. *Obviously*. She didn't say this, but I certainly understood.

She put out her cigarette and I finished my bottle of orange Oasis. On the gray windows of the group of buildings that climbed to the sky, white clouds slid, floated, doubled their volume, broke apart before fusing into clouds of strange, distant, unexplored planets. They penetrated the simple geometry of the windows, advanced like an unseen gas, like the smoke of a fire, agonizing, invasive.

We continued the interview with the little guy from the village circus.

'So, sir, you have brothers and sisters?'

'Yes.'

'How many?'

'Two.'

'Two what? Brothers? Sisters?'

'No, no, three.'

'Three what?'

'A brother and a sister.'

'And the third?'

'He's dead.'

'OK. Why didn't you say so at the beginning?'

'Uh... because he's dead.'

'How did he die?'

'The terrorists killed him.'

'OK. Are you married?'

'No.'

'Do you have any children?'

At that, the young circus fellow began yelling like a clown who has put the wrong mask on. Indignant, he wanted to know how she could ask him if he had children. Didn't he just say he wasn't married? The protection officer tried to understand. What's the problem? I sidestepped the socio-moral debate and told her briefly how it was impossible for him to imagine children without marriage.

'Well, it's not really very difficult, is it?' the officer responded.

We wiped the slate and moved on.

'Did you work before coming here, sir?'

'No.'

'How did you support yourself?'

'My father had a grocery shop. I helped him in our grocery shop.'

'OK! Then you worked with your father.'

'I didn't work, I'm telling you. We had a grocery shop. Sold things... uh... items... uh... things to eat.'

'So you did work in your shop!'

'I didn't work. I sold things.'

'How many days a week, sir? And how many hours a day?'

'From Monday to Sunday. Closed on Friday. From 8 a.m. to 10 p.m.'

'You worked a lot in your grocery shop, sir.'

'I'm telling you that I didn't work. I had a grocery shop.'

Now the officer was looking at me, at her wits' end. 'Is there a problem? Do you understand each other? He understands you? Or is there a language problem?' He understood me perfectly, I assured her. Maybe it was the word 'work' that was bothering him. For him, working meant being an employee. He was a shop owner. Someone above those who worked, who worked for others.

'Right, OK, we'll let that go... Otherwise we'll never move on,' said the officer. She hit 'Enter' with her index finger, its nail damaged from typing so many corrosive tales.

'What made you want to leave your country?'

'Terrorists... everywhere... they harass us... I'm Hindu... the fundamentalists torture us...'

'What incident forced you to leave your country?'

'Uh... the terrorists... the fundamentalists...'

'For what specific reason did you leave your country? What did they do to you? You need to be specific.'

'A young woman in my village. She killed herself. That's why...'

'What does that have to do with you?'

'Well, she was Muslim. She was keeping company with one of my friends.'

'Again, what does that have to do with you?'

'Uh… my friend was Hindu. Like me.'

'But, sir… how… How does that make it your problem?'

'This girl's brother was a terrorist in our village. He had beaten up his sister's boyfriend. He forbade him from seeing his sister. And the girl hanged herself. And I was accused of murder.'

'But how does that make you responsible? You weren't her boyfriend!'

'No… but the terrorist and his men brought the woman's body and hung it from the guava tree outside my house.'

'Why? Wasn't there a guava tree at the other guy's house?'

I burst out laughing. I couldn't stop or translate the question for him. He stared at me with his round, stunned eyes. A laughing fit in front of a man in distress. I should have been red with shame. Bitten my tongue. Lowered my head to the table to hide my outburst. I thought of the misfortunes in the world; of my own misfortunes, things that had happened and things that might happen. Being hit by a car before I can eat my pulled pork and plum sandwich. A pot of flowers falling from a balcony right onto my head. Crushed skull, my phone rings right at that moment, I can't answer it. It seems that the flowers were set there in advance for my funeral. I die. I cry. I cry for the people who would have mourned me. Nothing worked. My body was convulsed with laughter as if a flock of sparrows were fluttering, spinning and twittering around inside my ribcage.

On the way home in the RER I remember putting my forehead on the window. An open book on my lap. From time to time I picked it up. Immediately put it back down. An empty can rolling from one corner of the car to another caught my attention. Stations flew by. Sometimes the platforms were at the same level as my face, sometimes my feet. On the train car's pink wall, using thin blades, someone had etched a person's death, someone else had carved out their love. I didn't think of anything, of anyone, except a woman who appeared in front of my closed eyes like a fountain of light. Her face accompanied me the entire trip. Lucia was one of the protection officers I worked with sometimes. She wasn't the promise of a sexual adventure; she was as undefined as a landscape at dusk, a snowy mountain peak dusted with a pink glow, inaccessible, an unfinished dream, a sleeping desire.

By the time I got home, I was an empty cage buffeted by even the slightest breeze. My brain demanded a rest. Turn off the lights in the apartment, turn off the computer and mobile phone, turn off everything inside my brain and keep my eyes open, like this night in the dark cell, wide open like those of a goldfish blowing bubbles in the white pools of my own eyes.

Dealers of men

Life is a monologue. Even when you think you're making conversation, only a stroke of luck allows two mono- logues to intersect; perhaps taken by surprise, they halt in front of each other. In the offices questions and answers intersected but remained isolated. The men stuck to their monologues. The women officers shot question arrows almost automatically, lethargically and without a target. A few rudimentary questions later, the tension would rise among us. The tension sometimes rose so high that, long after having completed an interview, everything trembled deep inside me, throbbed like the engine of an idling car. The man avoided her gaze, I stared at him, she bit her lip and anger rose in all of us like nausea. We got annoyed seemingly over nothing. He out of shame, she out of weari- ness, and I, tossed between shame and irritation. Because I also remembered the land of clay, the eroding country, between the teeth of the ferocious water, the voracious bay, the water black like the tongues of the cruel goddess Kali, who swallowed up acre after acre. I remembered the mutated towns and the dusty villages, the lush villages with woods so dense that farmers sometimes had to chop down branches to forge their way through. I remembered the black earth, tender, soft on the banks of rivers where the roots of trees wove together. In the mud, in the water, children played, they caught tiny, slippery fish which waves had carried to the sloping banks, the sun causing the fish and mica-sprinkled mud to sparkle, the sun-silvered fish shimmering on the water up to the invisible line where the bay and the low sky merged into one.

The piss-yellow walls of the police station toilets begin to undulate. The room seems to breathe in each beat of my heart, each of my breaths, like a sponge. Nothing is moving in the corridor. The darkness is breathing like a sleeping monster.

In this silence I can hear the constant footsteps of people. They are from a land that has broken off from the continent like a gangrened limb. They are from a land that has been severed by the blow of a political axe. They first invaded the streets and sidewalks of the neighboring city on the old subcontinent. The record for poverty was broken. Living skeletons were photographed. Teresa, the Mother, the generous one, came to save them. But the old subcontinent wasn't enough to contain these assaults, to contain these waves of men.

Because, even crueler than politics, their own land then betrayed them. It crumbled into the bay, the water swallowed it up. The land was going scuba-diving. Six months under water, six months back up for air. Fields reappeared like the back of a giant, ancient tortoise.

So men wanted to leave. They learned to swim. They filled their lungs with air and dived into the water. Smugglers guided them to the other side. A corrupt, slimy, wretched jungle book. From port to port, their distant brothers were waiting for them, they pocketed their money, crammed them into boats, into planes. Their nets were made of iron. Immigrants were caught in them like shimmering fish that were transported and sold from market to market. These are the slaves of the new millennium. The blacklist is as long as the kilometers they have traveled.

Adam-byapari, one of those men told us one day. I translated – *dealer of men* – for the officer, and a shiver ran down my back. The dealer of men had also brought him to this shore. We encountered this *Adam-byapari* in other stories. He is the one who has a dozen legal businesses and others less so. The one who is in real estate, in tourism, in the iron and steel industries, the one who serves as intermediary for the purchase of a SIG29, the Russian warship. One of his many businesses is to send men abroad, *to deal in men,* said the petitioner. Men who are scrawny money machines, cash cows; hungry mouths awaiting them back home. The meager welfare assistance they receive in European countries is a windfall for their families. Once they are sold, the transaction completed, these men are scattered across European cities. A pair of Gap jeans, a new shirt, a fake leather jacket don't hide the stench of hunger. The clothes are merely a disguise so they can hide in the crowds of the cities of the rich. European dreams, white dreams which dirty hands, black hands, seize as best they can. Their country gone up in smoke returns in nightmares. It loses everything, its soul, body, blood and breath, it becomes an idea, a ghost of its former self. It no longer exists.

And still the migrating people continued to move from the south ever farther north, and when the north of their own country, the north of the near limits, was no longer enough, no longer welcomed them, they crossed the red lines, looking to the distant north, the north of their dreams; they went where they had no right to go. The tension increased in the room. Words wouldn't convince anyone. The men sweated, stammered, crossed and uncrossed their fingers, repeated the questions as if they were answers, silently recited sentences, their Adam's apple rising and falling, the words gurgling in their throats, stumbling out, pale and frightened. Words were added to words. Files piled up. An endless procession of men. You could no longer distinguish their faces or bodies. Together like a huge dark heap they made us uncomfortable. They had to lie, to tell a story that was entirely different from their own to seek political asylum. They took on the burden of a life that was completely foreign to them. They attempted to slip into the skin of people created by the dealers of men, their countrymen. Obviously, we rarely believed their stories. Purchased along with the journey and the passport, they were going to yellow and crumble into bits along with so many other stories accumulated over the years.

For a long time after I had left those offices, at night, the words came back to me at home in my empty room. Incoherent babbling filled the space, overflowed. Some nights I awakened suffocating, as if I were drowning in the rising tide of whispering, murmuring, and shouting. In my half-sleep I saw faces and bodies emerge out of the floor tiles. Blissful, intrigued, tormented people. They appeared when I blinked my eyes. Disappeared when I blinked my eyes. Like this night, in this police cell. To tell the truth, I am still not rid of that shouting and whispering.

The land of clay

'Let's go back to the place you left, to the place you fled,' Monsieur K. said to me yesterday during the first round of questioning.

'You can never go back to the place you've left. It's no longer there.'

'What is no longer there?'

'The place, of course!'

'Why is that?'

'The space has moved with time. It is the impossible geometry of life.'

'…'

'It's like the stars sailors see. With every assault of the waves they are thrown farther away. Their stars drift away. The place and time move. That point of departure, the port and its boats, that space is buried deep in your memory. It is nowhere. It will never return. The knots are undone.'

'Never any regrets? The choice you made seems right to you, then?'

'What do you mean, regrets?'

I told him how I remembered an afternoon sitting on

the banks of the river. It was one of those autumn days when you could dip your fingers into the light as if it were honey. I had recently arrived in this country. Everything I tasted was delicious. It masked the morass of administrative paperwork. I had sat down on the riverbank, facing the sun, facing the green stalls of the *bouquinistes* on the other side which were waiting patiently like so many fairy-tale frogs. My legs were dangling over the water, which was gently flowing by as I whiled away the day, when a voice called from afar, from the opposite bank. It was so precise, a straight and clear line, from one side of the river to the other, that I couldn't be mistaken: 'Mademoiselle! Mademoiselle!' 'Yesss?' I shouted back, and I could see two figures. Two men. One was young, very young, barely a teenager, and the other less young, more like an uncle who had taken the boy on a walk on a sunny day. 'You're not planning to jump, are you?' The concern in the voice reached me despite the wind and the distance. 'No, not at all! Not today,' I answered, and our laughter soared above the water.

'It's always like that with the people from here: I am facing their river, their lives, close to them, but against the grain. Yet they understand me, they talk to me with a sort of cheerful kindness, with the tender concern one might have for a puppy.'

Monsieur K.'s eyes wandered for a moment, then as if to conclude came back to me.

'You never miss it? Never homesick?'

I had stopped rocking my chair. My feet were flat, perfectly still, on the ground. As if I had nailed them there out of shame. Remembering drew me back to the land, to the obscure knots of the past. I wanted to bring Monsieur K. with me. With devious pleasure, I wanted to see him affected, moved, destabilized.

Homesick? It was the country that was sick. The memory of ancestors. A grandmother's tale. Old currency passed from one generation to the next. I was now passing it on to Monsieur K. A memory from the other side. *Opar Bangla*. I told him how, shortly before the bloody days of independence, people had left the country. Sniffing the situation like noble dogs, they had sensed the danger. They had fled the confrontation between the freedom fighters and the colonists backed by their police and their army.

Memories had to be invented. With the help of the smell of blood and gunpowder. I told him about the explosions: train tracks, telephone poles, police stations. I asked him to imagine the men who shot at white officers getting out of their cars. It seems they sometimes missed. Officers' wives and daughters in evening gowns, a teenage son holding a tennis racquet, they all crumbled into pools of blood, soon attracting the late winter flies.

Memories also had to be learned. Schoolbooks explained how the authorities had tried to divide the region, the hub of pro-independence movements. How, at the beginning of the last century, militants had managed to thwart the division of the region, and how, forty years later, at the time of independence, when each side was trying to quell the violence, the country, a single body, was mutilated. How that fertile land was pillaged, humiliated, persecuted, and ultimately cut in two, drawn and quartered by the colonists' great steeds.

Fairy tales mutated into tales of fire. Several years later, while the rain beat into the wooden shutters, while lamps were swinging and giant shadows danced on the walls, you could almost hear the *Allah hu Akbar* and *Jay Hind* shouted from the two religious camps, Muslims and Hindus: renewed confrontation every night. The monsters and demons of the tales had been replaced by fanatics who attacked each other on the streets with axes, knives, daggers, bamboo sticks, and pistols. It was said that people fell like banana trees. They also said that the Surabardi police finally decided to declare a state of emergency when there were no more bullets in the rioters' pistols and abandoned knives stuck out of the scattered bodies. Peace came in wobbly steps, with its vulture wings, dark, stifling; a peace that reeked of death, mute and dazed with shame. Daggers don't just slice skin, but reveal our own inner ugliness, flesh opened and spread before our eyes, nothing is forbidden, the frenzy begins, time stops. Killing is intoxicating. One can no longer go backward. Dead bodies pile up in one's memory. An insurmountable heap. With the logic of death established and practiced, peace seems unreal. How can you justify silence over mayhem and violence? Only exhaustion could slow those men down. After independence, after partition, for days and weeks, people walked from the other side of the border, their entire life stuffed into a sack on their back, their entire life suddenly cut off at the roots. The city's sidewalks overflowed with dead bodies and with bodies that were still moving, that begged, cried for water, for the liquid from the rice that is discarded after cooking, they didn't dare ask for more. From their abandoned kitchens on the other side of the barbed-wire fences, the smoke of all-consuming fires was still rising. The partition line sometimes went through houses, with the kitchen in one country, the bedrooms in the other. An apparently absurd division, yet very calculated. Cultivated fields in one country, factories in another. Programmed poverty for several decades. And people continue to migrate. To transgress. To go beyond the red line, where they have no legal right.

Heat surged up from the ground. Burned the soles of my feet. As warm as the rice juice that my grandmother gave to the dying on the sidewalk.

Still, it was bizarre! Not to ask for more. How does one ask? How does one emit the first shout? How does one shout for leftovers? Who can go backward, go back up the hill, become a man again after swallowing rotten leftovers fought over with dogs?

But this conversation had digressed so it returned to the subject at hand. Instead of taking me back to the place I had fled, my native country, Monsieur K. started to ask me about the way I worked. If I kept my eyes open. If I was always listening. Or if I was quite neutral in my role. If I wore my mask well. If I didn't feel smothered under that mask. If I hadn't wanted to pull it off, to throw everything on the ground and start screaming.

But Monsieur K. liked to let doubt, uncertainty linger, the freedom of chameleon words. Words that meant everything and nothing.

'Do you think you were patient enough with the petitioners?' Or, 'Would you have reacted with as much anger and violence if it had been a man from this country?' He cleared his throat and then repeated: 'A European, I mean.'

A white man, you mean, I snapped back silently.

His suspicions about me didn't bother me. He erased them a moment later with an indulgent smile. As if it were nothing. As if I hadn't attacked the man, as if I hadn't been indicted. Then he reversed and set a new trap for me. Left his sentences unfinished and waited for me to answer with a badly chosen word, a word that would fall into his trap. We advanced and retreated behind the mirrors of words erected as in an old theater where no one would dare shatter them. It was a low-budget operetta. Without a real ending.

I thought of another storyline, more secret, more tense. And yet so light that it wouldn't exist if I hadn't thought of it. Between Lucia and me. Lucia was all fire and ice. As an officer, she was formidable. All she needed was a whip and high boots. She yelled at the men, assured them it was for their own good, that she had to tell the truth, that it was the only way to help them. Then she looked at me. And it was impossible for me to hold her gaze. The blue of her eyes was exasperatingly beautiful. A blue-gray stone, semi-liquid, tiny imperceptible spokes of a wheel. With a glow that I guessed was white. I guessed because I never looked at Lucia more than a half-second. My head barely turned toward her, I would lower my eyes. And later, *now*, alone or with my friends, in a crowd, walking down the street, that glow came back to me, like a promise and a forbidden fruit. Maybe I attacked that man because of Lucia. All these men made me ashamed. And without knowing it I was leaning more and more toward those women officers who represented the law, righteousness, authority. I had passed to the other side. With a weight in my heart I had leaned toward those women who were exhausted by the constant procession of supplicant men. Women who were anemic, hollowed out, bundles of nerves. My tenderness for them was politically incorrect. Maybe I attacked the man because, in front of Lucia and the other officers, before us women, the man and those like him were actually an insult, an error, an accident. To me, their poverty didn't justify their bungled lives and lies, their aggression and their narrow-mindedness. At first I mumbled out my responses to Monsieur K. Then my voice gradually became stronger and I felt free and within my rights, for a moment.

'Do you think you have the right to fix singlehandedly a so-called untruthful system?' Monsieur K. asked me.

I didn't answer him. I lowered my head.

I thought about everything that remained motionless. The sidewalks are still as dry and cracked. The beggars, prostitutes and day workers talk in their sleep. A dog barks in the distance. The heavy curtain of night air doesn't move. I see them in the distance. In the distance I longingly contemplate my country that is spending all these years without me. These years of excess and abundance. These years of deception and masquerade. The slum dog wins the jackpot and the slum remains a slum. City workers bulldoze huts. Fathers sell their daughters. Daughters enter into the gaping maws of the cities. Child soldiers rummage through garbage, serve tea, pound iron, stop cars at intersections and wipe their windows, drag as well as they can the rickshaws whose seats are higher than their heads, run errands and wash dishes for the rich, break lamps and statuettes whose beauty is beyond them, sell vegetables and steal when they can; shop owners fire them, they return to the village, to the sidewalk, to the hut where they were born. They return to the maw of the devil. Child soldiers protect their homes with their matchstick arms. They fill their lungs with a great breath of air and dive into the dirty pool of rain, into the big holes in the sidewalks. The river overflows and drowns the city.

People, too. When the rain and the mud devour their

land, they try to run faster than the water. Sand covers rice paddies. People travel to distant lands. Looking at a sky covered with mist, they see new horizons rise up.

But laws remain immutable. Tectonic plates slide over tectonic plates. The canvas of the sky is filled with as many holes as an old circus tent. Entire countries are swallowed up in water, it is the future that is drowning. And herds of men still travel north. With their lies, their cheating, their awkward obstinacy, their dreams as sad as the rags on their backs.

Migrants survive despite everything just as rebel blades of grass grow in sterile ground. They always find ways to escape the blow of the sickle.

Nothing is lost, nothing is created, everything is transformed into images and dreams and nightmares. The night thickens in my cell like ink at the bottom of a well before the first glimmer of day.

The milky dawn softens the barred cell. The carnivorous plants twist their necks here and there in the half-light. My throat is tight. I have to throw up to open it. Crying has the same effect as alcohol. It is intoxicating. It empties you and makes you want to vomit. It annoys me when I cry for others.

Zebra-striped life

My memory was in shreds. I could no longer distinguish the truth from the lies that erase everything, that bedazzle. Truth and lies intertwined quickly into a dark knot of nerves.

Amid this confusion I wanted to understand how these men survived in their land of exile. How they dominated it. How they were dominated by it. I sought to know, more than I had a right to, I forced their hand, I listened and I heard. They confided in me, serving me tandoori chicken and *baigan bharta*, accompanied by puffy naans, in restaurants with latticework decor. They also confided in me in the interpreters' room. Those who had crossed the red line, those who had lived *there* and now lived *here*, they had so much to tell. They told me how they had survived in cramped quarters, hidden, imbedded into the secret folds of this city, rented with the last of their welfare payments. How could a dozen or so men live together in a tiny room? Far from the roofs where little terracotta chimneystacks stuck out like cigarette butts, their apartment buildings were carcasses where electrical wires hung, like severed veins, ready to catch fire. Days and nights followed the rhythm of odd jobs. Evenings were hectic. Flower vendors and restaurant workers left when the construction workers returned. Almost every evening fights broke out regarding cooking, cleaning, and sharing other household chores. Each person loudly exclaimed that he wasn't the servant of the other's father. In this country they are all orphans and don't know it. Things settled down after the meal and the main topic of discussion, the legalizing of their status, would begin. To remove the thorns from one's heart, the nails from one's feet, whitewash life whiter than the walls.

The restaurant waiters risked being told off by their boss as their memories overflowed, but they didn't care about the disapproving glances of the other; they some-times poured out *lassi*, sometimes their stories, for me. It sometimes happened that those who had women as bosses found those bosses particularly sympathetic. This gave them hope that they would be able to 'do the deed'. Their countrymen advised them not to let them get away, to get them pregnant as soon as possible. To be the father of a half-white baby, who would be born in this promised land, who would be, the irony of fate, the protector of his father, who would ensure the life of his father, here, in this country in Europe. And if, as almost always hap-pened in the end, the wives who were waiting for them back in the old country, tired of the rhythm of the rain and their husbands' letters, ever caused a problem, they needed only to send a false death certificate.

'You've really heard all that?' I asked the waiters. 'Just as you hear me say it now, *apa*!' Addressing me as they would their elder sister, they always touched their ears as a sign of sincerity. 'May God strike me down if I'm lying!' Then, settled once more, they continued: 'We have no choice, *apa*, what else can we do? Now our life is here. How can we leave? So we have to try.'

They try, yes, everything. Some keep bits of hot pepper and onion in their pockets to rub in their eyes when no one is looking to make themselves cry. Some arrive holding their baby and pinch it suddenly so it will scream and wail. They try to induce both compassion and tears.

Still, there was a place where the balance of power swung in their favor. The place of last resort for these petitioners: the court of appeal, following the rejection of their case by the office where their first interview was held. It was also a modern building, purposely understated, it seemed. Without the noble symbol of the allegory of justice. Without any symbols. Nothing gilded, no marble, nothing shiny or grandiose. It was a true barnyard. The gates and the guards were just part of the decor, anyone could come in and attend the proceedings. The crowd was often made up of those who had already jumped through the necessary hoops. Having attained the status of political refugee, they came to encourage their compatriots, advise them, protect them. They listened attentively to every word spoken in the room, every gesture that might be a sign of hope or of despair. Heads or tails. Their black gazes swept over those in attendance.

I watched them, too. But out of the corner of my eye. Our gazes must not meet. Otherwise another drama would unfold, silent, calculating. They would try to influence me, to make me feel the weight of their assembled community. I had to ignore an ironic *'salaam alaikum!'* shouted as a challenge after the hearing, after I interpreted, when the judges and the court reporter closed their files, their faces dispassionate.

But I watched them nonetheless. This one, for example. Or that one. Or another. There were so many of them and they were all so alike that I had the impression I was always encountering the same man. Neither their voices nor their gestures helped me to distinguish them. On the contrary. All together their faces and bodies formed a mass of black clouds in which a storm was rumbling. Words crackled out like disturbed waves from an old radio. Sometimes they stood up straight. Alert like hunted beasts. Sometimes from the outset their shoulders sagged. Crushed under a weight of fear and humiliation. Drawn between hope and disillusion. Sometimes they wept. In the name of their wives and their children. A dead father and an old mother. Their lips trembled. Their red swollen eyes filled with tears. At first they didn't want to cry. They bit their lips. Then they let themselves go. Crying did them good. Their arms lowered, their shoulders slumped, they cried and cried. They were offered a glass of water, a pack of tissues. Sometimes, after they had begun to cry, they realized the effect and cried even harder to convince us. I could have painted a picture of the various, repetitive pathologies, a tapestry of symptoms, new combinations. I could have kept a series of numbered, annotated records, as an attentive nurse might have done. I almost did it. Then the summer slowed me down. I saw things only through my own personal prism. Through a misty window. My own reflection surprised me, intrigued me. Like a cat, I wanted to put my paws on the mirror, dive into it, understand the image. Reality had the same mirror effect. *Lo spècchio. Il spettacolo.* A mirror always lends itself to spectacles. The others didn't suspect anything. It was enough for them to know I was saying the right words and the right sentences, that I remained faithful, that I wasn't using a pair of invisible scissors.

I kept my face neutral, mask-like. And I observed them. This one. And the other. All of them. Morning and afternoon. Sometimes late. Past lunchtime or closing. The security staff left, locking the main door. Inside, in the rooms, they stood up straight. Or often hunched over. Like that one. Or that one. I watched them and I wanted to understand how they used time and space. *Tusi-tala* number 61. Blue folder. Hope without color. He kept his head down. His hands in prayer. His round, dark profile, imposing, contrasting with his timid, frightened silence, with his submissive immobility. In front of the judge. In front of the ladies and gentlemen who, like pecking chickens, kept lowering and raising their heads into the piles of papers before them. The more they discussed his case, the more they argued, the more skeptical they became. They no longer believed his story. The lie became obvious.

However, he too had his own story. Like all the others. Touched up here and there to make it sound more authentic. His body the color of earth, the fertile clay of his country, a land crisscrossed by rivers, a land also often drowned, his body that perhaps still smelled of the mud and the wild plants, the freshly cut shrubs, was awkwardly wearing a denim jacket with a Union Jack flag on the pocket. Clearly, he hadn't forgotten his masters. Except he had knocked on the wrong door. In the wrong way. Too much bumbling and too many lies.

On his land the coconut and banana trees still bent under the force of the storm. Shredded banana tree leaves covered the village path like torn saris. The banyan trees resisted. Terrorists hid behind their branches and roots. The avengers. The plotters and the racketeers. We followed a fast-moving detective story. A political thriller. A story of violence. A gory, low-budget film. We discovered the hitmen of party A and party B. Those who set fire to farms and huts. Stole fish from the pond. Seized rice paddies. Hid weapons in their homes. Made false accusations against them. Raped their wives and sisters. Threw acid. Hacked off arms. Cracked skulls. Chased farmers off their land. Traces of their fleeing footprints in the black mud. Then one day it rained. Fat drops filled the holes in the mud, tiny ponds where the sky, low and overcast, could be seen.

The smell of rain had filled the room. The round, dark, imposing figure crossed and uncrossed his arms. Kept his head lowered. But in the official documents, they found no trace of fire. Neither his hut nor his village. The man and his lawyer painted the picture of the great fire – bridges collapsed, the sea in flames the mirror of the sky, the countryside on fire, red, orange, gold, the blazing portrait of a fascinating end. But the wager ended badly.

I raised my face to the room. Watched again the man who was seated on my right, facing the judge. His lawyer was standing straight, rigid. The language was clever. The body, sincere. What the words invented, the body belied. I no longer knew where the body stopped, where the language began. I no longer knew where the borders and barbed-wire fences began nor where the country ended. Where the trees stopped moving. The rivers silent. The fables and tales lost their innocence. The *tusi-tala* lowered his head. The lie entered his speech like water in the hinterland, its thousands of tentacles gripping the fleeing earth, the salty water, like the saliva of a monster covering the soft skin of the earth. One no longer knew where the water began, where the land was dying.

I had lost my old map. And my compass with it.

I had only the fables that were written behind the scenes, in the wings. Unbeknownst to me I had begun a personal inquiry. I was looking for the owners of this dark theater, the puppet masters who make these farmers dance and perform with such dexterity. Who bring them here, pay for their journey and sell them their tale, hire them for a thousand daily tasks and hide them behind the dirty curtains of their trade. A white van opens and reveals men piled up like slices of salmon, foreign and disoriented. Boats go down in the black water and the men still hang on, like ants on a floating leaf. The holds of boats carry men as well as baggage and cargo the way a whore hides her pregnancy and continues her business. They are lost children. Of the adult orphanage where oily broth simmers in the common pot. The room smells of cumin and burnt milk.

Smoke filled the room, we were choking. I wiped my eyes. Another lawyer/petitioner duo sat down. I put my right hand on the table. The lawyer took out a pile of new documents. She asked my advice on this file before the court. While my fingers were following the words on the pages, the man and his lawyer passed their hands over it. I couldn't help noticing my light-chocolate-brown skin next to skin the color of clay. I couldn't help comparing them. The resemblance made me uneasy. The difference in nuance made me uneasy. In the end, I couldn't feel at ease with these men. I pulled my hand away. Now white- and dark-skinned hands were passing back and forth over the papers.

The man remained with his head lowered and his hands locked in prayer. A Buddhist imbued with humility.

His voice was strangled and his gaze sought an invisible source, also inexhaustible perhaps. He began to weep at the mention of his wife. *The Islamist terrorists tried to rape her.* She was able to escape but not the young wife in the family. *My little sister* – this time his eyes overflowed and he cupped his tears in his trembling palms. She had been kidnapped by those men. A week later she had been found on the narrow muddy path between the cabbage and colza fields, her sari stained with blackened blood, her face beaten unconscious. A local affair or community reprisals, no way of knowing. Her body butchered, thrown in the mud like rotten meat. The clay-colored man wept at the thought of his wife and his sister. His cries shook the room. Real life poured into Buddha's palms, or perhaps another tale that distorted national stories so greatly that they intoxicated the listeners, making them cry, drunk with compassion?

The petitioners, Buddhists and Muslims and Hindus, lively or humble or sullen, the asylum seekers presented themselves as activist militants from various parties, the same stories and the same bodies blended in my head, lost all definition and all form, became a dark and shapeless mass of giant bodies, that growled, shouted, demanded, cried, pleaded. Were they inventing a new country, a new nation, unknown wars, hidden genocides? Following the lines of their sketches, the shades on their canvases, was like discovering a terra incognita, invisible and imploring. *It rains in that country the way we cry between the lines of history*. The canvas was faded. What remained after the downpour, the nuances of pale color, perhaps the meager truth, the only one, the residue, forgettable, forgotten the next day.

I'm going to tell you the truth

But sometimes the voice told the truth. Forced, trapped, stuck between the walls of absurd assertions, the man ended up telling the truth. But before getting to the bottom of things, the officer, the petitioner and I endured hours of serious comedy. The man who said he was a member of Party A and thus persecuted by Party B. The man who said he was a member of Party B and thus persecuted by Party A. The man who said he was Hindu and thus persecuted by Muslims. Or Buddhist. Or Christian. He was then asked what the most important holiday was for his community. Who were the gods and goddesses? What was his holy book? Who was the husband of Goddess A, who was in turn the mother of Goddess B, who in turn was the avatar of Goddess C? If he said he was Muslim and active in Party A or B, he was asked what the ideology and structure of Party A or B were. From that point, the interview resembled a hypnosis session. Ellipses replaced words. Silence wasn't golden, it was made of lead, it was heavy. It was the gray of fear. The man tried to follow an outline of simple sentences, subject, verb, object, direct or indirect. But the subject was related to an irrelevant action. The object was a

49

grumbling of indecipherable sounds. The man lost himself in his words as if he were in a Mongolian labyrinth.

It was at such moments that Lucia and I would exchange glances the way nurses do before they turn off the oxygen of a patient about to die. It was one of the rare moments when I could finally look at Lucia. Melt into her halo. Luminous, milky, Lucia reminded me of the ancient images of beauty, folklore, Greek epics, the perilous voyages of sailors and their tales. It is difficult to understand such aggressive beauty blended with such restraint. Her faded jeans and her thin-striped sky-blue shirt buttoned up to her neck. I thought of Georgia O'Keeffe's paintings. Female genitalia drawn as countless unmentionable flowers.

The men in the semi-opaque office, members of Party A and Party B, the men who believed in a god without a face and the men who believed in multiple gods, participants in a masked ball, always brought me back to earth. I descended from my cloud floating near the ceiling, basking in Lucia's perfume.

Sometimes we also witnessed the premature eruption of the truth. Both pitiful and funny.

I specifically remember a man claiming to be Christian who was asked to talk about his religious holidays. He hesitated. Licked his lips.

'I go to mass. I listen to the priest. I listen to everything he says. That's a holiday for me.'

'Where do you go to mass?'

'At the charge.'

My eyes widened. I must have looked like a frightened fish as I stared at him sideways.

'At the charge? What? Ah… yes, of course! Church! Is that what you mean? Church. OK! You attended mass at church. But aren't there other more important holidays for Christians? In the winter, for example…'

'I was always really busy… the terrorists threatened me… the terrorists didn't allow people in the minority to live… I saved my life… I didn't celebrate.'

'OK. But tell me a little more about your religion… For example, who came to see Jesus when he was born?'

'I don't understand!'

'There were some people, three people who visited Jesus when he was born. Who were those people?'

'I had a lot of problems, I was really busy, the terrorists threatened me… I didn't see who came to see Jesus…'

The man was clearly irritated. I bit my lip. Lucia glanced at me, checking to see if I was going to burst out laughing this time. I promised myself that I would do that later, but alone, in my bathroom, in the shower, I promised myself I would release the laughter birds fluttering inside me.

We met sellers of fish and vegetables, grocers and truck drivers who claimed to have pursued advanced studies at university. Fictitious degrees opened the path to a university life no less fictitious, which, in turn, allowed them to prove political involvement in student movements.

'So, sir, at what level did you study?'

'CSS.'

'What?'

'Uh, no, no, sorry! SCS.'

'Are you sure?'

'... HSC then SSC.'

Lucia already knew, but double-checked with me: SSC is the equivalent of a primary school certificate and HSC of the baccalaureate? Yes. So you can't pass the HSC before the SSC! No, obviously.

'Sir, what year was that?'

'In two.'

'Excuse me? Two what?'

'Two thousand and two.'

'Are you sure, sir? In two thousand and two you were thirty years old. You did your baccalaureate, uh, I mean your HSC at the age of thirty?'

'... No! No, no, no! It was in nineteen hundred and two.'

'WHAT?!'

I looked at Lucia. Lucia looked at me. He means nineteen ninety-two, I whispered to her.

There were so many things I wanted to whisper to her.

'OK, well... Let's move on. Tell me about the lawsuits that were brought against you...'

'Yes.'

'I'm listening...'

'I had a pineapple grove. The terrorists wanted my pineapples.'

'And?'

'Well, they were jealous of my pineapples… they wanted to take my pineapple grove… so they plotted against me!'

'And they implicated you in spurious lawsuits, is that it?'

'Yes, yes, madam, that's it.'

'So it was really a spat between neighbors? What is political about that?'

'It's political, I'm telling you.'

'How?'

'I was for my party. They were for the other party. So they were my enemies.'

'OK. How many lawsuits are there against you?'

'Four or five.'

'Four or five?'

'Four. Er, three or four.'

'Three or four?'

'OK, three.'

'OK. Tell me about them…'

'About what?'

'About the lawsuits.'

'Which one?'

'Whichever you want… Begin with the most recent…'

'In two thousand and nine…'

'Sir, in two thousand and nine you had already left your country. You were here… in two thousand and nine.'

'Really? No, no, they took me to court even if I wasn't there.'

'Why? How is that possible?'

'Well, they couldn't find me… I was in hiding… So they brought another lawsuit.'

'Who are "they"?'

'The terrorists, the police…'

'Ah! OK. How about the earlier cases?'

'In five.'

'Five what?'

'In nineteen sixty-five.'

'Sir, you are aware that in nineteen sixty-five you weren't born yet?'

'…'

'Sir, do you understand what I'm saying?'

'Yes.'

'So?'

'I don't remember.'

'OK. Right. A lawsuit for what? What were you accused of?'

'They were my enemies… I was active in my party… I worked a lot for my party… so they became my enemies.'

'No, sir, there has to be an accusation! What were you accused of?'

'Murder.'

'Who was killed?'

'Iqbal.'

'Who is Iqbal?'

'He's in the other party.'

'What happened?'

'We had organized a demonstration. They were jealous of us. They attacked us. They started shooting everywhere. And Iqbal died.'

'So this Iqbal, he was killed by someone in his own party?'

'Yes.'

'So why did they take you to court?'

'They were my enemies. They wanted to take my pineapple grove, that's why.'

Lucia and I had stopped for a moment, shattered, wiped out, weary. I wanted to console her, I forgot my own exhaustion, hers seemed insurmountable, unfair. It was always like that. I wanted to erase myself before her dazzling light. I spent my days swallowing my words at each attempt. I walked in the hallways, I saw Lucia through the window, I summoned my courage as I straightened the lapels of my jacket, buttoning it over my stomach, and I muttered a sentence, repeated it a hundred times, like a mantra. Lucia, can I buy you a drink? One day? The ambiguity of *one day* would have diluted my offer, my desire; it would have muffled that desire. In the end, I never bought Lucia anything. My infatuation embarrassed me and I always went back to the men of the city. I relied on their white, effective, sometimes even consoling bodies.

Back in the office we took up where we had left off.

'And the second case?'

'We objected about the first case. There was a fight.

Between us and them. A guy was killed. So they took me to court.'

And so, we encountered countless grocers farmers merchants whose goods had been stolen by terrorists. We also encountered countless heads of propaganda. Heads of such and such organizations, too. They all were. We also knew that they all had been to prison. Listening to them, one would have thought that there was not a single mere citizen left, and that the country, henceforth transformed into an enormous prison, comprised only valiant political leaders serving their sentences behind bars.

'So, as head of propaganda, what did you do?'

'I warned the people of the village.'

'How did you warn them?'

'I asked them to come with me.'

'Why did you join that party?'

'I don't remember.'

'Right, what is the symbol of your party?'

'Uh… I don't know how to say it… Can I draw it for you?'

'Go ahead.'

'There.'

'It's a wheel? A sun? What is it?'

'I think it's a sun.'

That day Lucia ended up telling him frankly that there was no point in continuing the interview because she couldn't believe what he was saying. She suggested he think about it, take a break. And added that he could change his story, that it wasn't a problem at all. She just needed to believe him. So he was questioned about his lodging. How was that going? And who was the man who was housing him.

'A brother. I mean, a brother from the village.'

'Someone you knew, then?'

'Yes. I'm staying with him. He feeds me. Also gives me three hundred takas.'

'Takas?'

'Uh, no, no, I mean euros, three hundred euros.'

'He's the one who gives you the money?'

'Uh, no, no, sorry! I give it to him.'

'And you work?'

'No. I'm not allowed.'

'It's written here "street hawker".'

'One day I brought corn. That's done a lot.'

'Yes, I know.'

'So, on my way, the police, those guys on bikes, uh, on motorcycles, stopped me. They threw the corn in the garbage and made a note in my papers. They also told me that if they ever caught me again they would take me to the station.'

The need for money forces these men to leave their country and their exile creates a new trade, the manufacturing of stories, of false documents – birth certificates and diplomas, memberships in Party A or Party B, doctored photos in which they appear alongside important political leaders. And in exchange they work for their saviour employers. A microeconomy in the big cities of Europe. A parasite clinging to the host body.

'So, you were the head of propaganda?'

'Can I tell you the truth?'

I couldn't believe my ears. Lucia had more experience than I. A Russian woman, born in Martinique, her first name that of a calendar saint. Her face didn't betray her thoughts. She was carrying three continents inside her. Fragments of those different lands must have shifted and jostled each other. I didn't know if she felt the earthquakes and tornados deep inside her.

I leaned toward the man like an amateur fisherman toward a trout that had come up to the water's surface.

'I'm a truck driver. I was going back home from the big city to my village. And on the way I hit a man. They accused me of murder. So I ran away.'

The man seemed both relieved and worried. He feared what was to follow.

I looked at his muscled arms, which he had crossed, making the muscles stand out more. A pale pink T-shirt clung to his torso and upper arms. The black of his skin gleamed under the fluorescent lights. Then I looked through the window. A woman wearing a short black dress was sitting on the tall wall of the courtyard. A man was explaining something to her. His chin could have touched the woman's left knee. Behind her were dense, manicured shrubs. She could have leaned back, let her head fall behind, lain on the bed of leaves. The truck driver had followed my gaze and was looking at the people.

'So? I've told you the truth.'

Lucia explained what would come next. It was routine. I knew it. The man didn't know it. We steered those people to tell the truth and ultimately did nothing with it. It was a dead end. We abandoned them at the bottom of the wall, at the end of the impasse, where hundreds and thousands like him, carrying their tales, piled up, stagnated, reeked, became scum among the scum, nibbled on by the worms of oblivion.

Those were probably the only times I became a bit angry with Lucia. She lost her mystery and became ordinary, devoid of magical power. A protection officer at the end of her rope. Ultimately powerless to do anything for these men.

The woman and man in the yard left. Rain was streaking the windows, leaving traces like cat hair. The sound of the rain drowned out the petitioner's voice.

Robin Hood

Then one day Robin Hood arrived. In my country, we call that type of person a *rustam*. A heroic thief. Tall, thin, bronzed by countless suns, he wore a heavy, gleaming silver bracelet, the smile of a cowboy. As soon as he came in he wanted to establish the rules himself, his right hand reaching out to us as a warning.

'Ladies (*listen up, chicks*), I'll talk first.'

'That's not how it's done, sir.'

'It doesn't matter (*I don't give a fuck*). You must listen to me first. All of that, what's written down, is crap. I'm going to tell you the truth.'

The officer of the day was a young blond woman with eyes as blue as a Swiss lake, new at her job, an angel, always appalled at the distressing stories of these migrant people. She was a naïve spectator in front of these dramas. She was assisted by another woman, one with more experience, shorter hair, whose facial expressions were openly jaded. We were all flabbergasted, amused by this charming hoodlum. The man said he wanted to protect his village from the selfish, ambitious, conniving, exploitative politicians.

'I invited them to have tea with us. I told them it was the first and last tea they would have with us and that if they didn't leave the village immediately after finishing their tea, they were going to have serious problems.'

Our *rustam* had left school when he was fourteen. At sixteen he had been stabbed in the chest. The attacker was his cousin, a young, strapping militant from a party, A or B, it didn't matter. On a boat one misty autumn evening, the knife was plunged between his eighth and ninth rib. Since then, he had traveled a lot. He had spent time in Italy, Dubai, Switzerland. The son of an illustrious family, *Sayed*s, today he sold roasted chestnuts at the entrance to a train station in the suburbs. And he was in love. A Tunisian woman. Who had passed in front of his makeshift stove where, on smoking embers, he was heating chestnuts and shouting '*mallonshaud, mallonshaud*'. So he absolutely couldn't be expelled from the country before he had found his Tunisian, whose name he didn't know.

The officers and I were nonplussed. A fit of suppressed laughter shook us from head to toe. We were biting our lips. We lowered our heads to avoid looking at the man. We did our best to hold it in. But the invitation to tea had already set us off. And we finally let ourselves go the way you relieve yourself after holding it for hours. Our laughter thrilled the *rustam*. He observed us for a moment, as if to test the effect of his exploits. We, young, out-of-control cockatoos, and he, a deft bird hunter, exotic and bandit par excellence. In another context, in a rose-gold scene, the three of us would have danced and yelped and done a striptease for him, wrapping our legs around the shimmering pole in a nightclub. The glass-walled room, bare and rudimentary, lent itself to this imaginary game centered around the tall, thin man who was sparkling with charm. For two full hours he took us on a boat ride, from one sun to another, from one dusty red landscape to another, he struck his hat against his leather pants with fringes on the side, then put it back on his head, covering his left eye, he chewed on a bit of string, then spat it out, his white teeth gleaming, he spoke little and observed a lot, squinting his eyes as if not to see the world head on. At first what he said was enigmatic. Gradually the mystery faded. In the end, he stood before us like a naked saber. He said there was no other far-fetched reason to be in this foreign country, a European country, except that he wanted a better life, that's all. Then he left, a cowboy at the end of a round-up, to return to his vat of embers and chestnuts in front of the train station. There was no glowing sunset around him, our laughter froze into embarrassed smiles. What emanated from us as from him was the pale glow of dawn when the heart expands like a magnolia.

A giant hibiscus

But the light of dawn did not always appear. My life at work had become an endless night. In this permanent darkness I once felt my body trembling from head to toe. From my belly there arose an increasingly irrepressible wave that ultimately crashed out of my mouth. A flower, petals spread out, red, a hibiscus. *But if it's red, that means I have tuberculosis!* I was drenched in sweat. I was at home in bed, staring at that giant red flower on the white sheet. I awoke with a jump, suffocated by the taste of dreamt blood between my teeth. But I was safe and sound. I wasn't the one who was sick. Actually, no one was sick. Even those who hoped to be. My dreams absorbed the desires of others, of all those who came to the medical center, where I also sometimes translated for them, people who were visibly disappointed when they received the doctor's verdict. The results of their physical were placed on the table. The doctor smiled at them, 'You see, it's nothing! Hey, what's the matter... you should be relieved, right?'

No, actually, they weren't. Quite the opposite, they were upset to know they weren't ill. Head trauma, malfunction of the nervous system, depression, the fallout from old bone breaks, hypertension due to being tortured, at least a bit of asthma, a little ulcer… But nothing, nada, nyet. Nothing to worry about! The doctor kept smiling.

In a lowered voice, that is, in a language that was incomprehensible to all these petitioners, a language that was a hidden hallway, a secret boudoir, the doctor asked me what was the matter. I told him what I could deduce from my experience: they wanted a medical certificate. Proof of a medical condition. For their asylum request? Yes.

'But they won't get one! There's nothing wrong with them. I can't provide a certificate just because they have a headache! And even if I declared that they were suffering from headaches… it wouldn't be of much use to them! It wouldn't be proof of their problems or the torture they say they have endured!'

The doctor was sometimes surprised, sometimes annoyed. Annoyed because these unfortunates awakened a disagreeable compassion in him. I understood.

'Should I tell them?'

'Yes, tell them.'

When I told them they would lower their head in despair, aggrieved that they weren't sick. Back with their clan, they would be berated: they hadn't even managed to cajole the doctor into signing a form stating that the black spots on their face and body were proof of attacks. Memories from childhood and adolescence, a little accident that had once made them laugh, could not be transformed into proof of reprisals.

Except for a few sessions at the medical center, I always went back to the other office. Carrying inside me so many stories, so much shouting, my head like a vulture's nest. I thought of all the words that I had never said to Lucia. But it seemed she had heard my silent speech. I followed her with my searching puppy-dog eyes. Briefly. A second later I buried my muzzle between my paws. She began to avoid me. If she ran into me at the vending machines she would call out to a colleague, touching the person's arm and offering to buy them something, a drink. I laughed inside. Then I got hold of myself. Because Lucia wasn't a burning question for me, nor even a certain answer, she was simply the rough outline of desire, of possibility. I had so much to do, I turned the page, I responded to the smile of a colleague, too, a man, always useful for marking the limits of one's flights of fancy. In the hallways at work, Lucia and I used the men who surrounded us to demonstrate our reciprocal, playful indifference. This game became so serious that I could no longer tell if it was real or a game. I unconsciously avoided Lucia, as I would any other person around me. I no longer sought her out. Then one day I sensed her gaze on the back of my neck, like a bluish light, a hesitant dawn, that gaze was joy itself, it created a blue halo around me and I walked away enveloped by its glow.

And always the men, in the hallway or in the

semi-opaque office, dragging us from our heights and nailing us to the ground, giving us a more concrete shape, more down to earth, we who were so dissipated.

On the other side of the computer, the man was motionless. The fashionable faded jeans and dark blue, fake silk jacket mirrored the self-assurance in his voice and movements. He was wearing a tricolor Eiffel Tower pin. His hair was cut short, washed, flattened on his forehead. The unease began when he pushed up the sleeve on his left arm a bit and made some delicate movements with his fingers, *mudrâs*, as if better to articulate each word. His wrist was bare, thin, without a watch. His pink fingernails, beautiful rectangles, cut straight across, reflected health and his attention to his body. He claimed to be the journalist who had wreaked havoc on the pyramid of local power in his country. During the interview the way he looked at us showed his appetite for women, his scorn, too. His words flattered them while deep down he sneered at them. This game of disdain and desire continued while he spoke of countries, journeys, days and nights.

He told us: this country isn't his. Nor was the one he had left behind. He belongs to no country. He belongs only to himself. From one city to another, from one country to another, he remembers only borders. A mute wind arises in the emptiness. From both sides of the barbed-wire. He collects borders. He collects barbed-wire fences, the mute wind and the emptiness. He doesn't remember cities.

Or bridges or rivers. He doesn't remember buildings or cafés. Or people. His trajectory is that of an arrow. He counts the accumulating kilometers. From his village to another, from one big city to another, from his country to the neighboring country, from the sea coast to the port, the first and the next, he counts the kilometers and feels proud. Proud to be a survivor. His mental landscape seems to be a dry and arid land. Without trees or water. Without people. He is alone, a warrior. He sees the point of departure, behind him, far away, scarcely identifiable. He focuses on the line in front of him. He can only go straight ahead. He can only cut and burn any obstacle that prevents him from advancing. The same is true of the flaws in his story. He fills in the holes between sentences, between facts, between truths. He weaves a story and wears it. He feels as protected as in a coat of armor.

But in the middle of the interview, the little rebel lost his way. We never found out what made him collapse inside. A sob shook him. Just for a moment. He pulled himself together, bit his lip. He wasn't proud of himself. Furious, he was ashamed. He still couldn't believe he had cried in front of women. Proof of an illegitimate sorrow. Proof of his ruptured life. It was childish. It was already a defeat. To suffer in a country where he wanted to live whatever the cost didn't make much sense. Here, he had to hide his pain, he had to show other wounds.

We were all overwhelmed by exhaustion, by a sense of futility. Always the same game played in an endless loop.

The petitioners, the officers and I, all of us stunned, our brains numb and mouths stale. I see myself raising my red-rimmed eyes from the tattered papers that would end up gnawed on by rats, covered with larvae, swallowed up by the dirt and the mud.

The belly of the fish

When my brain was overflowing like a garbage bin, when it could no longer take another word, I sought silence among the men of this city. Where words ended and bodies began. I loved to see my skin graze theirs like a black pencil on white paper. They had the gift of wielding their bodies and mine in a way that made us speechless, mute, shaken by gasps.

But sometimes, on rare occasions, words invaded me in those spaces, too.

He lived in a converted town hall. It was the first town hall in the area. A nineteenth-century building. The narrow entrance led to an inner courtyard. Stairs with black handrails, with flower pots, went up and down. Green shutters, pale yellow walls, flowers everywhere, something Mediterranean about it. American tourists were having dinner at white wicker tables. A cat was whimpering. Rheumatism, the man told me. The hallways were narrow, yellow, edged in bottle green along the skirting boards, the closed doors did in fact look like those of offices in a town hall. His room looked out onto the courtyard. When he opened the door for me,

69

he smiled, looking embarrassed. 'It's very basic. It's a bachelor pad.' 'It's great! I love it.' I was sincere. This little space had grace and a sense of lightness. You could imagine a day-to-day life that was free, airy, one that followed the rhythm of the seasons. Yet that was only on the surface; clothes would slide off our bodies and fall onto the floor, leaving us naked within walls as white as fresh milk. He had learned over time to cloak himself in appropriate and courteous words. Behind the painted window of his face I imagined years of silence. Up to then he had been as open as a coffee-table book with me. 'Do you want to come over to my place for some champagne?' Whether a final cup of coffee or a first glass of champagne – the drinks changed, the endings were always the same. It was still light out. It was too light out. When he put his arms around my waist, his hands caressed me obsessively. Throughout the evening they wandered over me with such regularity that I thought my skin might peel off. *My parents raised dogs. The dogs had become their life. More important than their children.* He confided in me. And yet, I hadn't encouraged him to share. I just hoped that he would tire and stop. Then, I earnestly took his hands and held them as if I liked him. It worked. He was touched. It also worked while he made love to me. To brace himself he leaned against the wall or held onto a pillow, or even, probably for less practical reasons, grabbed hold of my hair or my hips.

I looked at the ceiling. The walls, too. I heard the

clinking of dishes in the courtyard. The cat was still complaining about its rheumatism. I already knew that this would be an afternoon to toss into my dustbin of forgettable encounters. To bury in my cemetery of stray and useless males.

While I was thinking about getting dressed and leaving, trying to come up with some sweet and polite words, some light and detached words, words like froth on a glass of beer, he put his entire hand inside me. This time it wasn't the mechanical stroll of an out-of-control robot hand, but that of a true terrier digging in the sand and mud. This time he intended to penetrate me completely and stay there forever. And just as you pull out and empty the belly of a fish, his hand suddenly pulled out my words. Words with the salty smell of blood, the smell of fish guts, words that he sucked and chewed and swallowed raw.

'I was thinking of someone else...'

'Of another man? Right now...?'

'Yes, I was looking at that wall, your bookshelf, that book by Stephen King... and I was thinking about being taken by another man... at the same time... now... here.'

'Really? You'd like that?'

His hand trembled a bit inside me, from unexpected pleasure.

'I want to. Sometimes...'

'What do you want? A threesome? Two men? Or do you like women, too?'

'Two men… Women, uh, yes, but I can't imagine the scene. I need a trigger… You understand?'

'Yes, I understand. And would you like to see me with another man?'

He wasn't pretending to be curious.

'No problem. On the contrary! You're free to do anything…'

'Wow… I'm spoiled.'

He turned over in the bed. Away from me. Came back to rub against me, wrapping his arms around me like a stumbling drunk grabbing onto a lamppost at midnight. Then he murmured, blushing: 'I know I like taking a man. But I don't like being taken. On the other hand, a woman, you, for example, if you want to do me, I'd really like that.'

'Do you have a strap thingy here?' I said in a whisper, thick with lust. 'Sure… I'd like to do that. It would be a change for me.'

I giggled.

These existential quests were as precarious as the season. Heavy as that afternoon. The philosophy of the loins. It was as if I had an erection. Levitation. Being outside myself. And that was enough. That man, an aging adolescent gorging on sex, stuffing himself, that man with a troubled gaze and the body of a whore, a young monk who has broken the glass and windows of his own body and has howled with the wild dogs of the summer night; he moved and repulsed me in turn. And more out of disgust than emotion I got up and let him plunge into me. Rather, I plunged into him. I moved backward and forward. It was neither love nor hatred, but excess. With each of my thrusts I erased the moment before, I erased the moments before, I erased myself. What I once was. With another man. What I would never be again. I had slammed the door. Blocked all pathways, the smallest trails. I would never again be able to return to the one whom I used to call *my boyfriend*. I erase myself each time I go to meet men in this city. It is my own form of nihilism. Nothingness is a magnificent festival.

And so, I existed in alternating universes, between a succession of dwarfed men who spat out the words they learned by heart in front of the computer and of secret encounters with the men who pulled out my words the way you empty the belly of a fish. A pervasive acrid odor surrounded both. I lived this way, stifling my thoughts of Lucia, which existed only through the forbidden. Those thoughts were so light, so volatile that they might have been products of my intense need for exoticism. For me, Lucia was a promise of peace, a promise of relief. Of a belief that one day my wandering would be over and I would be able to surrender myself to her the way one returns to one's native land. That is, never. What's more, Lucia was only Lucia's body. I didn't know anything else about her. I needed so little. Over two beers with thick foam I liked to talk about her with my men friends as if I were admitting something that had never existed, was therefore invented, a blond invention.

I like life to be like that. Groping. Seeking. Stumbling. Like a blind Uma Thurman in a detective story. There would always be an Andy García to kiss me at the end. Life always takes us in its arms. Life is porous and triumphant, too. As fertile as a happy cow. Among the holes and the abysses grow plants, grass, bushes. Insects scurry at the plants' feet. We survive thanks to insignificant beings. Life is much more generous than we think. Life smiles at me in the mirror. I smile at myself, radiant, after sex. Life is tasted in small bites and it whispers little obscenities to me, it embraces me before the last metro home.

My mother's hair

Then another summer arrived, slowly but surely, and with it came the lightness of clear days, even inside our offices, beyond the city limits. Yesterday I wanted to tell Monsieur K. the story of a particular man, an asylum seeker among so many others, who nevertheless reminded me of that noble, majestic, and radiant sky.

As soon as he entered, the room was infused with a scent that I couldn't immediately identify. While he was sitting down, pushing aside the glass of water on the table, I imagined him to be a young shepherd, a buddy of Krishna, his body was a cloud of rain, dark and dense. And I finally recognized his scent. The smell of the hair oil my mother used to use, the thick red juice of the hibiscus. The smell floated in the room, increasingly thick and dense, it descended to the ground, then at the man's slightest movement it rose again and continued to float around us. Yet, we were not in a valley of cows where a film of silence is broken only by the prickly sound of crickets. We were in one of the semi-opaque rooms where glass separated the tales from various countries. Dusty countries and sandy countries, river valleys and the water's open thighs, perverse and debauched, arid, red plateaus, mute steppes and deserted streets where lazy flies buzz around a pool of blood; here they were all separated by glass, dampened, framed, recorded in Word format on the computer in each room. The sun beat on the windows. The officer of the day was someone I rarely worked with. She was impressed by the hibiscus scent, by the words the man spoke. I listened to him and inhaled that scent. A waiter then owner of an eatery for workers and bazaar merchants, poorly educated, his words less brilliant than precious stones, but precise and well cut. He talked, and I was transported to an evening in Cox's Bazar. The round, bulging lanterns, smoky, waving in the summer wind. An impending storm. The river's embrace becomes increasingly strong and the sea tortoises return to land. There, in the glass-enclosed room, the man with the cloud body spoke of attacks, plots, injustice and riots, narrow channels between two rice paddies filled with blood. The computer screen overflowed. I didn't know what distinguished this account from others, but the man's voice was modest, poised, what he said rang true. The officer glanced at me briefly, happy. After six thousand, seven hundred and fifty files she was finally faced with truth. She could hardly contain her joy. I guessed the reason and I, in turn, was overjoyed. We exchanged glances, complicit and delighted. We then advanced with small steps, soft and muted, as if toward a newborn infant; we were going to meet the truth. We rocked it, cuddled it, pampered it. From one question to the next we helped it grow, walk, say its first words. We were true midwives. Out of blood and sweat a man was born, a good man, a true man, and we were ecstatic to have been involved.

Eleutheria, freedom, defines the possibility of going where one wants. Whether human or beast, the desire to go where you want remains unchanged. Whether Greek or not, free, you are not. And they weren't, not one of these men we saw in our offices. They never would be. But they would be free to say what they had to say. They would be free to say what they wanted to believe was their truth. To speak is a freedom. Small, but even so. But Liber – the god of wine and free speech – isn't waiting for them at the end. They couldn't care less about the Latin meaning, they couldn't care less about flourishing, blossoming. They define their freedom as they can. To go where they want. To grow as best they can. Stunted, misshapen, half-blind, piled on top of each other in basements, they grow at night, take root in a land they do not like but which they desire.

And sometimes, a man among all these men arrives like a digression, time stops, hope begins. You might say that he has understood the secret movement of roots, the moisture of the soil, its cultivating embrace, you might say he has met Liber.

I raised my smiling face to Monsieur K. But under his mask not one face muscle moved. The light weakened along with my courage. My stories didn't add up. Weak, disjointed. Suddenly I feared they would never convince Monsieur K. of anything at all, not of my agony sitting in front of those asylum seekers, nor of my tiredness, not even of my sad anger. A shiver went down my spine.

Chechen Eve

And I told myself that she would never have grabbed a bottle to hit a man. Her thoughts were the complete opposite of mine, but as a counterbalance, like two halves of a circle, our thoughts met and completed each other. Like the two parts of the number 8, our thoughts drew a circle and returned to the point of departure, to the center, they came together. At the center, willingness. Genuine and generous determination. After she left Argun, a town in the hollow of a valley, after she left the country, too, crossing the border and abandoning the hilly land of Chechnya, she ended up at a potato market. From university student in Argun to potato-seller in Saint Petersburg, she worked during the day and at night slept on stuffed and lumpy sacks. Her Caucasus mountain-dweller features and her Russian ID card surprised people. They couldn't place her. At the appeal court, in the interpreters' room, that of the language jugglers, she would stretch her arms over the back of her chair and cross her legs like a seasoned and proud trapeze artist. Her body would form a T. With her eyes closed, she would tell of her days and nights among the potatoes. Along with her we imagined machine guns lying between piles of sacks, like punctuation marks in a long and meaningless text. With her arms like the white wings of an angel, she wanted to protect the fleeing Chechens. With her words, like nail polish, she would cover and color their raw, sharp, battered truths. Here, everything was in the language, in the words, between the lines. The name of a river erroneously placed next to the name of a village, a vague adjective describing an incident, planted like a knife in flesh, bits of sentences uttered under one's breath, a voice extinguished, out of fear, expectation, despair.

The future is in the hands of words, in the heart of the tale. You have to be able to paint the landscape with vivid colors. You have to know how to revive the moribund theater with the strings of puppet words. Ava, the Chechen Eve, a ray of light in my mother tongue, the blue vein of her throat swelling with emotion. 'On the way back, between two RER stations, I threw up,' she said, and burst out laughing. Vomiting, suffering, being sick for weeks, all of that was obviously nothing when it was a matter of protecting one's people, helping them, using this system of political asylum to improve the human condition. Manipulating the story. As a charitable act. She was the novelist. And an activist. With her, the good wars would never stop. I no longer knew how not to defend the men from my ancient subcontinent. My armor crumbled. My neutral soldier's mask fell. I listened to their stories, my eyes clouding up. Tears of distress and shame. Their lies made me blush. But I tried to locate the paths and emergency exits between their words. If only in the entanglement, the confusion of their sentences, as in the interwoven, jumbled-up roots of native trees, I could cut and create a redemptive path. The petitioner doesn't grasp the language of the court, he hears only its tone, elevated, determined, almost complicit. He relaxes. His black eyes shine. Here, you must strike hard, strike true. He returns to the race with a new set of stories. He wants to keep adding and adding to his words, his tale, his life, like an awkward tailor who embellishes his fabric excessively for fear of not providing enough. The balance is upset. The truth has something to do with aesthetics. What is dirty and vulgar, clumsy and crude, doesn't seem true. They lie out of a proclivity for excess. Out of a need to fill in what is fundamentally lacking. Lacking somewhere. Between the capital and the border. Between the tiny rural land and the thousands of dollars paid to the smuggler. Between the dream of the Boulevard des Maréchaux and sleeping in the dank basement among piled-up bodies. A dog barks. The heavy, serious curtain of night doesn't move.

The glow of Chechen Eve challenged my night, both motionless. Good wars and the not-so-good ones completed the circle. Sometimes we looked at each other, we smiled, in silence, in empathy. Never had the journey between the bay of an ancient subcontinent and the mountains of Central Europe been so short and so intense.

To love is to betray

Weariness overtakes my body. I can sense I am giving in more and more to the depths of this endless night. Neither anxiety nor expectation can hold me up. Beneath my leaden eyelids the monsters appear again, those I thought I had left on the restroom floor. Frightened, tormented, outraged faces, or worse still, those that are extinguished, lifeless. Everyday men and women demonized by their excessive emotions, their disquiet. The lines of their faces shudder. The shapes of their bodies take on the scaly lines of the walls of my cell.

Out of the mass of monsters two beings emerge. They get closer and closer as if they recognize me. Themselves unrecognizable, so utterly has their misfortune destroyed them. They purse their lips, it seems they are trying to tell me a secret, but no sound comes out. Those sad grimaces are enough for memory to open its armored doors. I then remember an infinite road, like grief, at the end of which they are waiting for me. They are both waiting for me in front of the entrance to a garden. Gray, dusty, raggedy. Still excited, they can scarcely hide their joy at seeing me. Trembling like the autumn leaves that cover the ground in the newly barren garden. I set down my suitcase. I am clumsy, I know, in the middle of this garden, my eyes are blurred, and I don't like my blurred eyes and I'm clumsy. I walk toward them. I don't recognize the lifeless and bloated face of the woman, nor that of the man who is so skinny he is shivering. He is the last leaf that clings to the branch before giving up and falling. The man and his shadow. I try to remember the face of the woman from before, beautiful and radiant, whose gaze is now damp. She approaches me, hesitates, steps back, and then offers a weak smile. An embarrassed smile, wanting to be forgiven, to be excused for having changed so much. Already, I feel odd being here, with them. With a heavy heart, uneasy, I drag my suitcase onto the veranda.

Night invades the house and its garden. Finally, I lie down on the sofa in the living room. Dark, heavy chairs appear in the room's lugubrious light like hippopotamuses wallowing in the mud. We don't move for a long time. For a long time our three bodies remain completely still. We watch each other in silence. Then our words erupt. We talk for hours. We speak and we realize that we absolutely cannot understand each other. They absolutely cannot understand what is happening to me. We talk to fill in what is fundamentally missing. We talk to overcome our fears. Too much time has passed, it is planted like a knife between us. Time has cut the cord. Only tiny scattered threads remain for us to hang onto. Shreds of words, stories, we cling onto them, we slide, we fall, and we smile, awkward.

The two of them, there, my parents, sitting across from me, their eyes glowing like embers in their hollow sockets, their bodies trembling with emotion. They haltingly seek in my face, in my body, in my spoken words and in my hidden thoughts the proof of our connection, like the basic equation of a mathematical formula that is now too complex. They are in turn confident and cautious. They have only snippets of memories. And the present prevents them from hanging onto them, from putting too much faith in them. Like a gust of wind I sweep away their confidence. My presence is the sign that our connection has been broken. Unease rises in me like nausea. Very soon, so does anger. To see my parents is to go back into the murky water of my mother's womb. It is to be reduced to darkness, to the obscure and dangerous combination of two bodies, to the weak chain that connects them, a tadpole. To nothing. The more they try to catch me, the more they reach out their arms, the more I escape them, stubborn, unbelieving. It is a conflict between blind memories and the need for a future, the need to become someone else. Gnawing crabs of suspicion prevent me from believing I am connected flesh and blood to these two crumbling bodies.

I imagine his penis, hanging like the gray-black tongue of a slaughtered steer. I imagine her vagina, the opening as slack as the useless fold of a giant wrinkled fruit. Life has damaged the features of their faces and bodies as if an old potter had lost his touch. Life has distorted the words that once rhymed as in a fairy tale. Life has been upended by a devious chess player. With each word, with each gesture, I anticipate and move and capture their black pawns.

In my parents' house, among the sleeping hippopotamuses wallowing in the room's dismal light, our words flourish like green plants in the brown bubbles of filth. That flourishing of words is almost biotic. From my European city, often seized with a sudden urge, I would call them. A biological call. I realize that they would also call me out of a biological habit. They also realize that I no longer understand what is happening to them. We have remained with our primal habits. Rather, we are *reduced* to our primal habits. Forgotten, that which was learned, acquired, over time. Forgotten, that which had been discovered, the familial microculture, the story of evolution, collective survival. I have forgotten the weak circle of light cast by the evening lantern, smoky, the soot collecting on its rounded shade, the smell of overcooked rice, soft and sticky, glued to fingers, a mother who lost track of time and ran to the kitchen, throwing down the novel she was reading, I've forgotten the golden yellow of the soup, the weightless, dancing kanji of the steam above the pot. The wind was shifting in the adjoining room. Since my grandmother's death it smelled like wet cotton, and from the black depths of the copper pots rose the green odor of mildew. The town was silent around the house. The spotted dog, white and black, a nervous mutt, barked from time to time. Tearing the virgin veil of the night.

If to love is to understand, then incomprehension will quickly turn into hatred. The hatred I imagine in their eyes is my own. My stubborn rejection of their truth.

Death restores things. It fixes and sanctifies them. But terrible is this life that continues, crawling, this decomposing life, bodies and words, thoughts and gestures. I can no longer recognize myself in it. I no longer recognize my parents.

My father's voice is choked. Like wind rumbling in a tunnel. In between words, the air that chokes him tries to free itself. He coughs. He resumes his rhythm. He doesn't answer me but asks new questions. Fixed observations. He throws out sharp-tipped sentences to mark his territory. It's a wall. He protects himself behind it.

Father, blue shirt, white shirt, you don't wear them anymore. Your golden body, bronzed by the August sun, your athlete's body, you only needed a pole, you jumped, you made it over, you traveled through the years laughing. I spent the afternoons on your back in baby steps, my toys in the hollow of your body, in Mother's flowing hair, the hair of a sweet sorceress, who always cut my nails too short, forced me to drink steaming milk, smelling like a cow, Mother, even when I was a child I knew we weren't mirror images, your face as if from another clan remained distant to me, I didn't recognize Father, Grandmother, in it, their signs of affection, your arms hugged me tight, almost suffocating me, your tears sometimes flowed down my back and I shivered without knowing what to do, mainly not knowing why I should do it. Father, my little mother, I don't love you, I didn't love either of you. If today my voice is loving, it is because I know how much I don't know how to love you. I used you like a rocket uses a launch pad, with my legs pressed together I gave you a kick and I propelled myself into the void. Straight ahead.

The public swimming pool

Life is a public swimming pool. Dirty and full of intruders. You bump into those you want nothing to do with. I said that to Monsieur K. when he asked me about our lives, those of the interpreters, coming from various countries, how we get along together, what we have in common, how we clash. From then on, I didn't mince my words with Monsieur K. I talked to him as if I were thinking out loud.

In the interpreters' room, a confused cacophony of languages. A cluster of different, obstinate vehicles at the intersection of the world. Voices like strident horns. You were almost getting used to it when something else came crashing in. Little groups formed and grew here and there, breaking apart as some were summoned to work. I, too, moved like a tectonic plate, breaking apart, dislodging, detaching myself from one continent to join another.

The performance began in the morning. Some were loud actors with a great dramatic range. In a series of anecdotes, they unveiled the secret of the profession to us, the conflicts, the scheming and the little calculations. Others were Greek heroes and heroines, spokespersons for the oracles. So splendidly calm, they lounged in chairs and let the day flow by without comment.

In the middle of the room, the daily picnic of the pigeon-girls, chatty and famished. Some of the men had left to walk four kilometers under the August sun to eat halal and discuss Derrida. Others, less intense, chose the bistro next door to eat pork chops and discuss Audis.

The hours dragged on heavily.

People left and came back, weary.

One slept with his head on the table and raised it if a new discussion somewhere in the room interested him. His glasses stayed on his bald, shiny head. I was afraid they'd slip off, but they never did. An old habitué with his old glasses.

Someone else was looking at his computer screen nodding his head, the pink wires of his headphones bobbing along with him.

Two girls were talking about a synthetic folding bag being given out free at the local Franprix. A third girl was trying to convince someone to go with her to get one.

From time to time, they all shot me a reproving and defiant look, sneering at the book of the day under my nose. Sometimes it surprised them, sometimes annoyed them. *Always with a book! What is she trying to prove? She buys books to prove she's rich!* They were never very subtle. Especially when the mystery of what I was reading bothered them. It was as if I were practicing a rite from an accursed cult without regard for the others.

We were always waiting. Wilted like tired lettuce that had stayed too long in dressing. Waiting. An interview. More waiting. We were all hanging together from the worn-out rope of our endless day. We would buy chocolate bars, cans of Coke and Sprite and other junk food from the vending machine at the entrance, as if we were on a break, as if to cut up time into thin slices, then prop the thin slices up and watch them collapse like dominoes.

Then one day, a day that had begun like so many others, lunch was interrupted by an outburst from Mariam; she was talking faster than fashion, wearing a cap on her yellow-and-blue headscarf, African foliage surrounding her round, black, shiny face. A juxtaposition of fabrics. Juxtaposition of centuries. Mariam had found a sweet and submissive, almost pious woman to rant to. A forty-something woman from the Caucasus. Her thong was sticking out of her low-cut jeans, which revealed buttocks as white as the glaciers of her country.

'But he kiss me on my lips. He my nephew, OK! But on my lips? A nephew? That's disgusting! Isn't that disgusting?' Mariam had been in a heated discussion about AIDS and the use of condoms with her compatriots from Mali, Mauritania, Gabon, and Somalia. Spread out, majestic, on the blue vinyl sofa in the corner, she kept pushing up her big black-rimmed glasses. Her transfixed opponents formed a circle around her while she argued, sweeping away objections with a wave of her muscled hand as if she were cutting through tall grass. Booba, very worked up, tapped his right temple with his index finger and repeated one long sentence punctuated with incomprehensible profanity: 'But you have to be sick I don't do that, but if that happened to me I would ask for a moment and I'd put on the condom and if you don't agree then madam come back another time but I swear they have no brains in their heads the people who don't use one you have to be sick you have to be sick!'

Booba walked around in circles as he spoke, the others tried to calm him down and bring him back inside the circle, but he kept going around in circles and his ideas along with him. They smiled indulgently. Like a slightly loopy big kid, Booba was now tapping both his temples with both his index fingers.

Lying on the other sofa opposite that constellation of black stars, I occasionally raised my eyes from my book, its white cover embossed with vertical stripes. For a while now, I had been distancing myself from Asia and was gently sliding toward the dark continent. I didn't always recognize their faces or remember their names. But this wasn't a problem because in fact from one greeting to another, from one 'four kisses' to another, I changed arms like a baby among her nannies, and the chaos was nothing but affection. Maybe in these women I saw a welcoming mirror. We joked about the percentage of cocoa in our skin. The difference between sixty and eighty percent didn't distance me from any of them. The girls from the East, from countries each poorer than the next, always stayed like solid butter high up in the pantry, golden and precious. One or two of them sometimes approached us, like old village busybodies who spy on their neighbors' every word and gesture, surviving on the crumbs of suspicions.

'But, Booba, why are you still repeating the same thing? We agree with you! We already know all that. Who are you trying to convince?' I teased him.

As if turned off by a switch, Booba stopped short and didn't know what to say for a few seconds. Mariam burst out laughing and the others chuckled.

'You're going to go far in life…' one of them said to me.

It was my turn to be quiet, embarrassed by that generous sign of respect. It wasn't because I was humble, but because I wasn't sure what the person meant by 'go far'. It is quite possible that our sense of the distance and the journey are not the same, I said to myself, and I picked up my book again.

The rubbish bin was filled with food wrappers and also with notes from interviews which the interpreters threw away, not only because they were supposed to, but also out of irritation. The sound tore through the damp silence. The black plastic bag was filled with wretched tales from borderlands. The summer became difficult. One lost any notion of leisure or of a normal life. Within this structure of iron, glass, and wood, life was an eternal battlefield. Some felt guilty about making money off these poor miserable people. New debates took off. We were each the special envoy of our country; our reports remained on the drafting table and it was forbidden to remove them from this arena. Some also sought to redeem themselves, to rid themselves of the burden that weighed on their souls by *helping* the petitioners. 'I don't give a fuck about neutrality. I don't give a sh... Ah... You know what I mean! Those are my people. *My* people. They're suffering. We can't imagine what they've gone through. So I'm done with being objective. I'm saying what I want to say.' In another life, I would have easily taken him for an enlightened Maoist. In fact, he was little more than a boy, as light as a twig, with a hollow belly and a bony, badly shaven face, out of which emerged his big, blazing eyes. He was an illegitimate knight for whom no crown of flowers was waiting and who also didn't know which grail he was seeking.

In another corner, near the window, I thought I heard a name which, like a golden coin, was passing from one hand to another. So I pricked up my ears. It was the name of a writer from a desert land, from an arid spot on the planet which Soviet tanks had abandoned a long time ago. *The Patience Stone* annoyed the shallow-water swimmers. *He wrote to please the people here. It's not like that in my country*. One of the fish said. *That's obvious! He's a brown nose. He wrote for the West. What the West wants to read about us*. The other one followed him. Big bubbles came out of their mouths. That cartoon image didn't amuse me. Not patriotic enough, only rusty knots in my head,

I didn't know how to fish in this muddy water. Irritation has something corrosive about it. I must have put a cookie in my mouth to stop myself from speaking and to ease my burning stomach. Contradicting them would have only pushed me farther against the wall where I often found myself, alone and suspect. In those moments I was between several high walls of glass, trapped, lost. My feet dangling, my cry inaudible, my claws scratching the glass. And the others, with blindfolds over their eyes, turned in circles around me, fought, fell, got up, and knocked against each other, around me the lands of wet clay melted into the sea, pirates surged from the water, child soldiers raised their machine guns high like school trophies, black niqabs enveloped bodies and faces, soot covered entire countries and suffocated everything else, because poverty, like beauty, like life and truth, is to be suffocated, buried, because poverty is a state secret, and a stone was waiting, waiting a bit longer, before being launched and shattering these high glass walls around me.

The female knight and the mullahs

Madame Baumann wasn't the only one in the group, but to me she embodied all the chivalry of the court. She was a tall, heavyset woman with short curly hair, like little black shrimp covering her head. She would lower her large black-rimmed glasses and look over them. She seemed to be permanently scrutinizing and judging the entire world. She pushed her glasses up when she argued her cases. Inspired, sweating, she was the warrior who was fighting for justice not only for her Asian clients, but for all of humanity. Her stubborn strength seemed to come from a more secret source, from between two fossilized layers in the history of her people. At the other end of the table, completely at odds with her, I remained petrified with stupefaction, hypnotized by her words. I was stunned by her ability to lie, by her complete absence of scruples. Her tactics mainly consisted of attacking the interpreters, accusing them of not having translated what her client, the asylum seeker, had said, and constantly ordering them to choose such and such a word, which obviously didn't have anything to do with what the petitioner had said. Like a petty caid, she tried to impress us, to frighten us, us interpreters, the most fragile of tools, the least protected in this factory of lies. It was as if she were chewing us up and grinding our bones and scornfully spitting out what was left of us. She interrupted everyone, including her client, claiming to correct what in her opinion was a serious misunderstanding. Thanks to her, the borborygmi of the petitioners became the emotional speeches of a politician. These sellers of vegetables and rice themselves seemed embarrassed, disturbed, overwhelmed by the glorious role their lawyer attributed to them. They stammered and mumbled, their voices so low that they disappeared entirely in their throats. But the presiding judges and their co-magistrates often had the sensibilities of rhinoceroses; their thick skin protected them. Or they were like old porcelain taken out of the cupboard for a holiday; unfamiliar with the commotion and misery of the world, they didn't say a word for fear of being broken. They were jaded from the interminable requests of these people who didn't convince them. Among the experts and the judges, there were also those who took fifteen minutes to locate on a map the countries where the petitioners had come from. Their eyes wide open, they swallowed the tales of crimes the lawyers recounted. It was popular theater, chaotic, shrill. Stories completely made up.

Men cried, raged, pleaded before the court. Once they had left the courtroom, they threw their costume and mask to the ground. Immediately surrounded by a crowd of countrymen, they described their performance with hilarity and pride. People demonstrated their approval or disappointment, depending. The lawyer joined them and gave them their grade. Congratulating them on their acting or scolding them if they had failed. In fact, she had no luck with these people. More than once she was forced to reprimand them. I ended up feeling sorry for her and her ilk. They had to play their part and they didn't have the option to discard their costume or mask. They were knights riding around in the fog, without a goal, pretending enthusiasm, persuading themselves they were defending a great cause. Each time rekindling their inner fire; it probably required a huge forest fire of an eternal summer. I would have liked to question them. Especially Madame Baumann, soften her up, buy her coffee. Good coffee. Not the cat piss that flowed out of the vending machine. See her in the tender afternoon sun that shone through the bay windows and get to know her. Far from the brouhaha of the court where petitioners hung out, petitioners from all the so-called *developing* countries, a word chosen to help people believe in change, to convince people of evolution, since poverty frightens not only the poor but also those who are nice and warm. You would be wrong if you thought the rich like perpetuating poverty. That's not the case. They prefer seeing the world evolve, not too much ugliness, not too sad, above all no dying like an abandoned dog taking its last breath on their doorstep. They are content to have an easy and cheap workforce for their many tasks. Pay workers just enough to convince themselves they haven't sold their soul to the devil. They push away the devil and push away poverty, far from their doors. Otherwise, time would seem to stop, frozen; condensed into a dark mass, it would float around them like a bad omen.

Even so, there was a place where the petitioners felt at home. The Association that welcomed them, advised them, consoled them. A shelter from the downpour of misfortunes. An oasis in the desert life. I managed to find it one Friday afternoon. The metro took me to the end of an interminable tunnel a few kilometers from the City of Light, to a neighborhood where the concrete walls, cracked, broken, revealed their iron carcasses. The sidewalks as cracked as dead men's teeth. The streets, weary and leprous, went off in all directions.

Coming out of the metro, at an intersection, I was lost. No landmark. Around the square there were shabby reproductions of the same cheap and hideous merchandise. The piss-yellow sky didn't make matters any better. The entire neighborhood was an open-air bazaar, an open garbage bin. The violent wind slapped me hard. It continued to strike me as I walked. Dirty paper and plastic objects were flying around. The merchants had spread out their wares everywhere, overflowing onto the sidewalks, into the middle of the street, as if the many shops around the square weren't enough. Clothing, bags, suitcases, shoes, and a pile of shapeless objects, enough to fill the chests of the dark queens of this neighborhood at the farthest edge of the city. It had the air of an abandoned work site. It was a ghetto. Another country. The one I had managed to leave behind. It was impossible to believe there was still a luminous city not very far from here. The metro had brought me to the end of the tunnel at the edge of the world into this land of rubbish overrun by outcast jellyfish. Men roamed in herds here and there. I continued among them, caught by their hostile, ensnaring gaze. From time to time snippets of what they said reached me.

I had walked just a short distance when it started to rain. A heavy, vicious rain. The wind made it worse. With my umbrella broken, I tried to find shelter in the narrow doorway of a building. An African man had reached it before me, but he immediately made room for me beside him. On the street, anarchy ruled. People were packing up, covering, putting merchandise into boxes. At dawn, hordes of animals had emerged out of their dark caves, their secret cages, to sell their wares. With their apparently common features, the citizens of the global village, all together yet each so alone, now scattered and wandered off. Each a world unto himself. Each a unique world, a chaos. McDonald's burgers and faded jeans democratized appearances. Deep within, insomniac volcanoes rumbled. I looked around at the scene, not fully present. I was feeling increasingly irrelevant and out of context. My presence was a mistake on a cartoon drawing by an inept artist.

The gray, weeping zone spread out like a bad omen, hostile and mean. Poor. Poverty incorporated like a contagious illness. Under control. Quarantined. In the ghetto. This poverty irritated me. Its ugliness made me sick. If I could have, I would have turned around, taken the first metro and returned to my own neighborhood, where the smell of good baguettes blended with that of yellowed books placed in boxes in front of shop windows. There on the streets dogs walk with their owners, the café owner jokes with the couple of daily customers, brown-and-green cast-iron tables and chairs lean on the slope of the sidewalk, red-and-white checkered tablecloths flutter in the breeze. I simply wanted to erase my character from this ghetto cartoon.

The rain stopped. People came back out from visible shelters and from hidden caves. Immediately seizing her chance, a woman wearing a shiny blue-black turban and a boubou of the same fabric, completely soaked, plastered to her mother-body, shouted in a little nervous voice: 'Corn, corn...' She looked like a mother overwhelmed by her purchases, who had stopped under shelter because of the rain. I saw no trace of the mentioned corn, probably hidden among her bags.

I continued walking and finally found the Association. Life here suddenly slowed down. Buildings rose up around the courtyard. You could see refugees doing housework through the large, uncovered windows. Some were resting, chatting on lounge chairs in front of their doors. Concrete flagstones laid on patchy grass led to an entrance at the very end. The Association was a space of respite for those who were tyrannized elsewhere and everywhere. For once they could gather in a place where they were listened to. A few young women and others who were less young were fidgeting and flustering around them like mother hens protecting their chicks. They were teaching them the ways of refugee life, advising them, telling them about various sources of state-provided aid. They were the avatars of Mother Teresa. Except they hadn't seen the famous Calcutta sidewalks. Living far from the chaos, far from the din, they imagined a country and opened their arms wide to save it. These golden nymphs had the milky hearts of young mothers. Their affection overflowed, feeding the fledgling hope of these people. There is joy in nursing the poor and unfortunate. Charitable work soothes a guilty conscience, eases the burden of debt one has toward others. We feel a bit more human. We are less afraid of mirrors.

We act out of guilt. From one era to another, from one corner of the world to another, we attempt to erase injustices, the crimes of the past. The fascinating geometry of time and space always gets ahead of us and we commit new errors. We believe we can balance the scales, correct the anomalies in a country, in a time; new anomalies arise elsewhere.

In this welcoming space the petitioners were allowed everything, or almost everything. They were advised not to lie to the authorities, but they laughed, inexperienced and unbelieving. They thought they could pass through the holes of the net thanks to their talent as actors. Eyes were closed to their faux pas. No one criticized their lack of curiosity about this host country, the language that always remained foreign to them, except when they blurted out two or three words to claim their rights. They left their ghettos only to return to their points of departure. Protected by invisible armor, they traveled around this country. Their language, their customs, their habits remained intact. Nothing and no one could take this from them. Nothing and no one could alter their thinking. They carried inside them their land, their fatherland, their religion. They were the scattered lands of a nation that continued to exist because of them, in movement, in suspension, like castles in the air. Invincible, impenetrable, opaque, their castles scattered in and around the city.

One day, they had unanimously agreed to support the fatwa decreed by the mullahs of their country against a woman writer, a compatriot, in exile. They had brought up the affair, comparing me to her, suspecting and denouncing the writer's influence over me. Indeed, I was the shrew. The stepmother in the fairy tale. I told them that their Allah had never once given them a hand when their carts had become stuck in the mud, when the smugglers had extracted astronomical sums from them, an entire life's savings, when they were sold stories, the total package, were forced to work illegally, for a pittance, for

102

they were as they were, diminished men, broken men, men piled on top of each other in the bitter stench of urine and sweat, waiting for sleep like drunkenness, waiting for dreams like the dazzling white that erases and swallows everything.

The social services angels didn't approve of my behavior. For them everything was permitted when it was a matter of survival. These daughters of revolutions, of the Paris Commune and the Resistance knew better than I that truth is relative, that lying is relative, that in the struggle for existence honesty is only a luxury and that before arriving at Judgement Day, there would be many rounds of Russian roulette when truth and lies, integrity and villainy would merge and be as one.

Those women felt uneasy with me. What we are, alone, we no longer are in a group, in a gang, swallowed up by the masses. We become something else, under a different mask, a different shell. The crowd has a single rhythm, a single breath, a single gaze. It uses its slicing power to cut out the tongues of individuals. A uniform entity, it feels invincible and because it is invincible, it demands uniformity. What bothered the people around me was perhaps my inflexibility both in the crowd and in solitude. I remained the same. I was the one who tore down the concrete structures of ideas. I was the reverse side of the image. The anomaly in the logic of death and poverty. My body, too, belied the pitiful image of my country. The theater of charity was halted because of me. They were scandalized by my skirts and dresses and my shampoo and my brown boots, which were considered arrogant in the building at the end of the courtyard. They wanted to put me in the mold, to dress me in the habit that makes the monk, to shed a tear for me out of the corner of their eye. But I didn't bend. My cheerful dresses continued to fly like the flag of a better life.

Monsieur K. stopped asking me questions. I wanted to tell him how I had learned to avoid poverty, to turn on my heel, to burn bridges behind me. I wanted to tell him that those people, too, had left their countries like rats deserting a sinking ship, and that in the end, I understood them.

The wisteria woman

And so, that was how I spent my days, chewing on thoughts and counter-thoughts, until the moment when everything shifted.

At first, it was a face like any other. Lost among some thirty men gathered in the room at the Association, ready to receive the advice and sympathy of the guardian angels. At first, it was a dark mass, then the mass moved, a hand rose up to speak. The oval of the face as dark and somber as the cloth that enveloped it. The slow, shy nature of the gesture revealed the femininity hidden under the hijab. Shefali is the name of a flower. The flower-woman, the wisteria-woman, wanted to talk alone. We weren't supposed to do that. Even if I was her quasi-compatriot, my role was limited to translating the words of everyone, no more, no less. I explained this, my mouth dry. In front of me, she uncovered her face. Burnt. Black on black. A scorched landscape. Calcified skin. She held my arm. A shrunken hand where the snakes of burn marks slithered. 'It's like this everywhere, you know, my entire body,' she told me. During the break, I took her into the hallway. What she told me made me take her into the adjoining room. Her mother had died when she was six months old. Her father remarried. Then it was a Cinderella story with a bit more violence. The stepmother tortured her, deprived her of food. She spent her long days doing housework. School was an amusement park where lucky children went. Not boys and girls whose mother had abandoned them, exhausted, haggard, bloodless after giving birth. When she was ten, her stepmother, now thinking only of her own children, kicked her out of the house. She began to work. A laborer, a cleaning woman even before she was a woman, a waitress in tea stalls. She stayed for a long time in a brick factory where the workers constructed their own buildings, low and narrow, around the furnace, with bricks that were deformed and overcooked. At night, the circle of bricks around the courtyard lit up with an orange glow. The orange glow in the strange dark night was a UFO which never managed to take off from the ground, from a land that instead swallowed it up along with its passengers and their dreams. Life continued. After the brick factory she worked in a sari shop. Bathed in the scent of the fabric, nestled in its silky skin, she grew up. She discovered that clothes had a magical power to hide, to save, to protect. She learned to hide between the layers of fabric like an oyster in its shell. Then, the day of her twelfth birthday brought another surprise. One surprise hidden in another. And soon it was a Russian doll of surprises. Her father appeared at the shop. Took her to a restaurant to celebrate her birthday. Someone told the stepmother about this clandestine encounter between father and daughter. They decided to bring her back home; since she was earning a living, and not a bad one, she could contribute to household expenses. The little bit of money accumulated during those years immediately went into the stepmother's coffer. Then she was forced to marry, which could have been like any other forced marriage. Bitter and strange in the beginning, then softening, comfortable, even pleasant, over time. But for Shefali it so happened that her forced marriage was with a ne'er-do-well in the village who, through a perverse generosity, invited his pals to enjoy his new wife. To escape, she ran, stumbled, got up and hid in the stable. Then it was fire that ended the story. The straw and Shefali burned together.

I have never seen burnt flowers. It is probably easier to burn women than flowers. It is more exciting to render mute those who have a voice. Place one's heavy foot on a mouth as on a black hole and stifle the cries, as has happened since the first dawn of man.

Later, when I returned to the court of appeal, I found myself facing another woman, quite young, pretty, delicate. Her name wasn't that of a flower, but she was one, wisteria. Accompanied by her lawyer, she told the court, in front of the judge and the others, how she was the victim of a gang rape, twice in a row, and how she had wanted to raise her child, the outcome of the first rape.

Her lips began to tremble. The first tears appeared and pearled at the edges of her eyelids. Then she let go. She wept. She wept a torrent of tears. At that moment, she could easily have been compared to a flower damp with the dew of the early morning. Soon crushed, drowned by her own tears. Translating her words, next to her, my throat was tight, my eyes damp. I wanted to take her hand resting on the table, a hand she lifted from time to time to raise the bottom of her yellow-and-pink cotton headscarf to wipe her eyes. The entire room was suspended, holding its breath, for fear of too quickly and too violently freeing the emotion rising in her.

The next day, during a coffee and tea break, I told my colleagues about that episode. 'Ah, you've been had!' Veterans of the profession, they knew how impossible it was to raise a child of rape, they knew that rape had become the preferred and profitable crime of those people, that they put onions in their pockets so their eyes would burn. The tears that flowed down a face, the lips that trembled, the voice that broke, began to melt together in my memory like a watercolor surprised by water. 'Don't worry about it! You did the right thing. Thanks to you she'll get her asylum.' Chastised, but still moved by the memory of the tears, I sipped my mint-infused hot water.

But the night is a different matter. Between dreams and awakening, the gelatin of unconsciousness. What the day eliminates, the night appropriates. Dreams are where the wild beasts are freed. The roots of trees drowning in muddy water are enlaced and intertwined. Under the water, in the smell of the soaked wood and the cloying mud, grow the shadow fish. I am awakened in the middle of the night by my own cry. Or by the idea of a cry. I don't really know if I really cried out, if my vocal cords vibrated violently or if the muscles of my throat and my mouth formed into a grotesque grimace; from the depths of me a shriek was freed. I am propelled out of the blankets, toward the wall where there is the giant armoire with a mirror on one of its doors. In the midst of this nocturnal entanglement, I seem to be shouting at a figure hunched on the armoire. A pile of rags, dark blue, fear blue, a woman. The cry and the likeness of a woman, the likeness of a woman and the cry, two feverish images, confused, confounded, juxtaposed, ultimately vibrating together, my cry and my idea of the cry, the woman and my idea of a woman.

And so my nights were inhabited by the dryads and naiads of the burnt woods and black rivers of Kali's tongues. Something was permanently broken in me. Life had shifted to the other side, to the place where darkness, strangeness, fear reign. Crabs of doubt nibbled at my fingers and toes. The frightened women frightened me to my core. Their fear penetrated me; it entered into my secret rooms like a gas, like a cloud, swirls of fear invaded the night, advanced, enveloping me and smothering me. The morning light arrived like the disappointment of spoiled milk. In the metro and on the platforms, in the street, going up stairs and along sidewalks, I wondered what was keeping me from shrieking. I wondered what would happen if I cried, sobbed, crumbled, fainted. My restraint surprised me. My desire to shriek, to spew incomprehensible, dirty, violent words, was so strong and I was so afraid of myself that I kept myself on a leash, I held onto the key to my chest of emotions. Confused sounds rumbled inside.

So many confused sounds are still rumbling inside that I must now keep myself on a leash in front of Monsieur K.

Impossible geometry

Sometimes, my fear transformed into anger. At the end of an entire year in those offices, my life was divided in two: fear and anger. Maybe it was my anger that made me afraid. I was afraid of myself. One of those days, I left work, wiped out, bitter and irritated, and went home. In the big train station with dark blue tiled walls, with columns like banyan trees, where a mass of people in a hurry scurried in all directions, were swallowed by the deep sloping tunnels that went down to the platforms and the trains that vomited them up somewhere else, I counted my steps to follow a direct trajectory. I went through the moving wall of people with a single goal in my head: to not let myself be swayed by the others and to not change my trajectory. That others were getting ahead of me didn't matter. I just had to avoid going backward or veering off. And yet, the young, dark, brown, chocolate, pale, amber, golden, pink, coppery women, round like bottles of port, bowling pins, thin like unfinished sketches, in shorts and flashy tops, in flouncing skirts, in skinny jeans, in baggy jeans, accompanied by young men in tracksuits or in jeans that were falling down, in skinny or baggy jeans, who were running to their weekly meetings, managed to sway me and to make me deviate from my path. It was only just another of those assaults by anonymous bodies, I thought, when the man appeared in front of me and uttered a weak *excuse me* in his language, which I recognized, because without turning my head I knew he came from the same place as I did, or close by. I didn't stop. I turned to the right. Toward an open garbage can where soggy sandwiches were fermenting around plastic and glass bottles. I stepped away from it. The man was following behind me. He said *excuse me* again. Having followed me a few steps gave him the right and the courage to continue. 'I am not allowed to speak to you!' I said before stepping over the rug of a mute, kneeling beggar whose cardboard sign informed us she was hungry. In the past, I had also seen her spread out in prayer to an indefinite god, the scarf on her head brushing the filthy ground. I didn't remember if I wanted to kick that pile of black rags or pick her up, help her sit up straight. She could go begging afterwards! The man didn't step over the beggar's rug, he went around it, hesitated a bit then blended into the crowd. Disturbed, bitten by the little ant of a guilty conscience, I turned to look at his escape route, my steps moving forward, but, my gaze rerouted, I ended up crushing a pink plastic horse which emitted a death cry and crumbled, flattened, among the other steeds. Their seller-master rushed to the display to save the last of his two-cent cavalry.

A bit later, on the platform, as I was trying to put it out of my mind, the man reappeared in front of me like a column suddenly rising up from the ground. He was stammering. Nothing alarming in what he was saying. He had seen me at the asylum seekers' offices. Couldn't I give him some tips for his case, some advice that would make his request succeed, offer him signs to predict his future? My mouth was dry. My tongue was stuck behind my clenched teeth. The man on the platform could not accept my silence or my evasive words. I decided to teach him about life. The financial crisis and the suicidal traders, the literally immobile market, layoffs everywhere, offshore companies and factories, dislocated, anesthetized and euthanized, the obstacle courses of language, administrative papers, the rites and codes of a new tribe. My speech exasperated me. But the man with a file to be padded had skin as thick as that of his interlocutors in this foreign country. He had been temporarily halted but he propelled himself onward like a rocket in the black sky. He was less masochistic than I thought and saw no farther than the tip of his nose. This Europe, even through deadened senses, still inspired his dreams. Like the others, he had to learn how to tighten the knots of his story, transform it into a coat of mail that no interrogation could pierce. I glanced at him and the disfigured resemblance between our bodies struck me, as if he had cheated, as if I were seeing us in a fun-house mirror. The same clay-colored skin, his less shiny, probably lacking good nutrition and good moisturizer, his haggard eyes those of a stray dog, constantly begging, constantly desperate; his clothes enveloped him, looked like an old flag taken out for the big day, he emitted a stifling odor of curry, cumin, incense, and something else, the stench of poverty, which you can smell from a distance and which halts you in your tracks.

I stopped preaching. Also, speaking in a language that I use only for my work bothered me, even if it was the language of my mother and my father and the countless friends whom I had left on the side of the road, behind the metal barrier of the airport, between two oceans, in the gulf and under walls of coral. Memories still shimmer, fading in the black water like secret fish. The water swallows them up. I remain stunned under that deep water. Dazed and irritated as much by my speech as by my silence, the man left me quickly. He probably thought I had gone over to the other side.

Narco-pirate

But after all, who am I to talk about them? I am stealing their stories. I sublimate them in poverty and ugliness. I am a narco-pirate. I am trying to get high.

But in the People's Theater I didn't exist. My role was to erase myself. My entire effort consisted of not existing. That should have been just fine with me, because I was a frail presence, hesitant, scarcely an outline. I was the backwater hidden beneath the city. But it wasn't a matter of evaporating gracefully, of fading away silently. I had to bark for long hours so that my voice would drown in the pool of voices. The court and the office, two speech factories out of which the smoke of words emerged, words like the remnants of dreams, words like the bodies of unborn dreams, the factory wheels were going to crush me, reduce me to shreds, turn me to pulp. I was going to disappear.

There was one woman who manipulated the levers of the wheels and the grinders of the factory particularly well. This lawyer spent the day making the entire court wait. At the end of the day when she finally decided to appear in the courtroom, the judges and their co-magistrates were all exhausted, their heads buzzing with political tales from various countries. As for us language gymnasts, us trapeze artists, our minds were numb. The lawyer blustered in, followed by her protégés, the asylum seekers. Her frizzy hair was pulled to one side in a bun, dandruff constantly falling from her head, covering the shoulders of her lawyer's robe. From the black mass of her lawyer outfit there emerged a face and fleshy hands, all covered with eczema. Years of agonizing pleading and tons of barely credible cases had clearly taken their toll. After listening to her for months, we ended up believing that there existed an unknown country, a secret and distant land, loaded with bloody and stifled stories that she alone had discovered. In my head I saw a country parallel to the one I thought I knew, with new laws, new governmental and administrative rules, a new people and new rituals, habits, and customs; in my head there emerged a surreal country, a country like a castle in the air, a country that existed only thanks to the confabulation of that lawyer. Some interpreters couldn't have cared less about what they were hearing and translated without emotion. They talked to their friends, gossiped, smoked with the lawyers in front of the big bay windows at the entrance. Cigarettes left a bitter taste in my mouth and the cold wind slapped me. So I didn't leave the building to join them. The lawyer and I often encountered each other but only in the courtroom and, unlike Madame Baumann, her proclamations were surprisingly vicious. Her voice flayed my ears, it sounded like the sharp squealing of a train coming into the station, scraping the edge of the platform. I swallowed my irritation and pretended to be indifferent.

But last month, she took me into the hallway to speak to me one-on-one. The time had come to burst the abscess. She began to dig her tunnel of words. In a nutshell, she wanted me to translate in such a way that things would work out for her clients, that the fate of the petitioners wouldn't depend so much on the court's opinion. In a nutshell, she wanted me not to translate the hesitations and muttering, the contradictory statements of her clients, only the essential, which conformed to her own arguments, smooth sentences, as brilliant as the truth. Then she finished, ripping off her mask, shrieking like a wild animal: 'If not, you'll see! All the lawyers will turn against you! I'll show you what that means...' I didn't know what it meant but I was so shaken by anger that I couldn't say what I wanted to say, which was that I was planning to continue exactly as before. Our eyes met like two glowing lanterns swinging in an evening storm.

Nothing happened. Everything went back to normal. At least, that's what I thought. If you could always rely on appearances, I wouldn't be here, sniffing like a dog, trying to find the source of the yellow stench of mold in my police cell.

The night as confused as a blushing virgin

And I thought of Lucia. Yesterday, too. I was tossed around each time the metro braked and I thought of Lucia. Like a promise, like a password to a secret account, like a key to a treasure chest. Lucia wouldn't have penetrated me, Lucia wouldn't have invaded my space, she would have scarcely brushed my borders, the edges of my lips, she would have left me intact. She would live this love with me without changing me, without distancing me from myself. Loving her would be like looking at myself in a mirror, kissing the reflection. If I had been allowed to do it. If the man in the RER had let me go to her. If the man in the packed train car hadn't diverted me from my path. I wouldn't have been forced to grab the full bottle of wine. I wouldn't have been forced to hit the man with the bottle. The red wine wouldn't have poured down my arm. The red wine wouldn't have run down his head. His face wouldn't have been deformed by a hate-filled grimace. And I wouldn't be here in this musty room where since yesterday I keep drawing my family tree in my head, the lines of my thoughts and my wandering, to justify my trajectory, to reconstruct the scene, so they can understand the desire buried in my blood, my sudden desire the moment I hit the man, one of those immigrants.

My body was moving with the rhythm of the metro and so were my thoughts. I wavered between a *yes* and a *no*. I thought about all the triumphant agreements in Lucia's gaze and I wanted to surrender myself to her. As if everything had already been said. As if this get-together at her place were inevitable, relaxed, had already occurred. As if it weren't the end of the line, as if the line had no end. In my coat pocket I fiddled with the piece of paper, already crumpled from over-fiddling, on which she had written her address. The train was packed. The bag, the book, the cell phone, the hat, the bottle of wine, and me, all together we were like a clashing addition to a collage. My hat was too red. The fur collar of my coat was almost an insult to those people around me who were piled on top of each other, like a heap of filthy rags. They were going home from work. Drained, haggard, irritated. I was going to see Lucia. I was going toward a luminous thought. Milky. Peaceful. The idea of peace made me impatient. I hated the back, the bison hump of the man in front of me, against whom the brim of my hat kept crushing. I thought of Lucia's hair, her golden cascading curls. So completely different from straight hair, curls always fascinated me with their potential for unpredictability, for surprise. I tried thinking of her dressing gown, but I couldn't. I didn't have enough imagination. I saw her in her office shirt, which she would unbutton to the shimmering path between her breasts, to the hint of curves where a gold cross would dangle. I was again tossed and bumped into the backs of others, others were tossed and bumped into me, and I gently protected my thoughts of Lucia as if I were holding onto a little cage of sparrows in the crowd, against the crowd, afraid it would break at any moment. I was also afraid of my evening with Lucia. I was afraid of ruining everything with the banality of a rendezvous, with stilted conversation, with the potential mistake of the encounter.

And I was tossed again into the man in front of me. But this time it was someone else.

Barely touched, he turned around with that strength possessed only by people consumed by an obscure rage. First, there was a flood of insults. I met them with silence. Which became a challenge. Insolent. Provocative. More insults spewed forth. I'd had enough. I hurled away the cage, I threw away my thoughts of Lucia and the evening with her, I stood up to the man. From beneath my hat I told him to shut up. The man grabbed my fur collar and shook me and threatened me and suddenly let me go, his eyes wide. The good people in the train continued to read their newspapers or look vaguely out the window. I stared at the man, appalled. I didn't know what he had recognized in me. I didn't know what could be so recognizable in me. As for him, I couldn't tell where he was from.

It's strange that I feel the need to determine the point of departure whenever a foreigner is involved. About others, the blond, golden, platinum, brown-haired, dark-haired, light-haired, pale, pink, tanned, I don't ask that question. I don't wonder which region or *département* they come from. But about the man wearing tattered clothes, whose face reflected the color and features of his native land, yes, I wondered. Because he had turned toward me, because he had exploded with insults, because he resembled the thousands of people I saw in the glass-enclosed office, I wondered. I looked closely at him and I wondered. I wasn't really curious about him. If I got closer to him it was only to eliminate any possibility I might have known him. From under my red hat my mouth opened, but what followed was only a torrent of pent-up fury.

I didn't know the man but he recognized me. He remembered his ordeal, his humiliation, his distress in front of me, in front of the questions that poured out of the computer screen. He also remembered that he had approached me in the station, on the platform. Or maybe it wasn't him. It was the other one, the one who wanted to sell me a bouquet of roses. Or maybe the one who cried in front of us. Or maybe even the one who shouted and accused me of not speaking his language. The militant leader who couldn't stand up to the flood of questions, who drowned in them, who became angry, the militant leader who today was selling roses in the streets of this city. All these men who con us, who con themselves, end up perhaps believing their own fables.

His face blackened by rage, the man grabbed me again. He crushed the fur of my collar. I was worried about the fur. Not really about me. Because I already knew I was going to hit him. I just had to take the bottle out of its brown bag, let the bag fall to the ground, and grip the bottle by its neck. Bees were already buzzing in my head as I grabbed onto the bottle.

The rest is just bungled dialogue, an exchange between deaf mutes who don't use the same sign language, who have frozen fingers and faces. The rest is just an attempt to find the identity, single or multiple, of a single evening, of the day and the night, close to and beyond the barbed-wire fences, an identity that one changes the way one changes clothes. You shave your legs and along the way become another, you disguise yourself, you have a new skin, you hide under the new mask. The underground peoples live in hiding at the mercy of the great nation, flout the law, take advantage of the human rights treaties, and the poor become poorer, their lands swallowed by the thousand tongues of Kali, their lands surge up from the bottom of the bay, like the backs of giant turtles, the poor sell vegetables, spinach and radishes, die where they are, the militants who are right and those who aren't lash out where they are, kill each other, men fall like banana trees while small merchants sell their shops and pay the smuggler, pay for the journey, pay for the story, land in the European city, shout and cry and demand and plead and end up insulting the one who looks like them but who betrays them.

The black face of hatred was leaning closer and closer to me, our roles were reversed. Now, he didn't fear anything, now he didn't have to mutter his words before saying them, he could stretch out as much as he wanted, stretch out his arms, his hands, he could grab my collar with its petty bourgeois fur and pretend to strangle me simply for the pleasure of the act, only for the pleasure, he could allow himself anything, it was the point of no return, a zone of indifference, too, since no one in the train car was saying a word, he was nothing but a vomiting mouth, a shapeless lava flow, threatening, terrifying, fascinating, even, because I could do nothing but remain motionless in front of him, against him, with him. First, threaten him with my words, then raise the bottle. Attacking him was the best means of defending myself. It was leaving myself and going to the other. It was worse than self-interest. It was better than self-interest. It was at least showing interest in the other. And so I went to the other, to him, the man, I aimed at his head, it was at least taking an interest in his head, in his person, if I couldn't love him at least I could detest him, I wasn't ignoring him, I was attacking him, I wasn't turning up my nose, I wasn't acting like a well-behaved bourgeois woman, I reacted, I burned, I burned myself, I hated, I attacked, I went to the swamp, I slid on the muddy slope, I lost my map and my compass. Crossing the border has something irreversible about it that resembles mourning, a secret crime, a loss of self, a loss of reference, a loss of life.

The lizard in the sand

His smile is what I need to be most cautious about. Question after question, he would push me up against a wall that didn't exist before, that he had gradually built behind me. Monsieur K. had turned me into a cardboard character. One that suited his easy suspicions, a deserter like all the others, but who looks down on those like her. A woman in exile, so far from herself that she no longer recognizes her own. Her devotion to this host country is suspicious in its excessiveness. In its unheard-of upsetting of the order of things. Her love for one is fundamentally only hatred for another. She takes into her arms those she knows the least and repels her people to avoid looking herself in the eyes, to better distance herself from herself. Everything is transformed, complicated, passing through the twisted pipes of the still she has deep inside her, and what she spits out is frightening.

Sitting in front of him, in his office, I await the verdict. My body is rocking with exhaustion, impatience. Monsieur K. is waiting for me to shoot that cardboard character with bullets. But I'm the one waiting for the firing squad. The questions pierce through and the cardboard body full of holes billows in the wind. Monsieur K. pushes me farther into the wind, into the void, straight into the wall. I'm the one he attempts to create as his favorite character, his straightforward guilty one. The one who feeds on hatred, who pours it out in public. I suddenly sit up straight. After all, what if I really were who he thinks I am? A chill runs down my back like a panicked lizard running through me, zigzagging. What if I really were who I didn't want to be? I shiver like that panicked lizard.

And suddenly my back is up against the wall. I throw javelin responses at him, I bring him a few kilometers from this European City of Light, beyond the red line at the city limits, into the ghettos with the leprous streets where he will have never set foot where he will have never sent his daughter or his son to do an internship in any store where he will have never gone out to walk his dog where he will have never gone for a party or even a burial, people like him live and die elsewhere they have their schools universities offices bars cafés and restaurants movie theaters and nightclubs their galleries bookstores and libraries their hospitals and their cemeteries elsewhere far from where I take him in the rain in the mud in the suffocating stench of poverty where all the exiled live those who love and mourn their country and those who forget it with each sweep of the broom they pass over the sidewalks where my days live and die, and the night never ends, with roles reversed I put his head under the cold shower of words and stories the same that I've heard nine thousand five hundred and seventeen times the same that echo in my head which pound my head among the graffiti-covered walls among the walls erected between the cities and still the downpour of words that teem on the walls always too many words too many people who teem in the cities who pollute. Monsieur K. wilts in front of me, I want him to be as exhausted as I am chewing on the same words the same sentences until he ends up vomiting pulpy dried-out bitter words until there is no one to pick them up from the sidewalks until Monsieur K. is blackly bedazzled before my monstrous killer words hideous as the truth. At that moment, you don't give a fuck about aesthetics, you know that the truth has nothing to do with beauty, with clothes and with camouflage. I am naked before Monsieur K. In my opinion, he is too. Naked and shivering.

Then he turns to his computer. The mounds of files in his open cupboard, gaping like the stomach of a shark, risk tumbling out. The night collapses like ice floes. I remember a girl who discovered she had a nest in her hair. I tell about how I discovered I had a vulture's nest on my head. I no longer think about the sea or jellyfish-men. I think only of myself. Of my life that I see redacted and reduced on an administrative form. I see only one form that will free me from this room in this police station, dirty yellow like a moldy lemon. Like ants, the words will devour the blank pages, swallow the hideous truth of the incident and leave me alone with myself. A sheet of paper justifies my anger, erases the red wine, erases the sleepless night, gives me the green light to go wherever I want. A square piece of paper sums up my wandering. Where I'm going. Where I come from. My cardinal points. My trajectory. What I think. What I do. What I will do. Tomorrow. The day after tomorrow. And the day after that. In the years to come.

Dawn comes limping along. With a sky the color of spoiled milk. The fly that came into the room yesterday is still looking for an exit and bangs against the window.

I'm at the end of my play. At the end of the night. Walking off the stage I need a mirror. The walls are naked and yellow. My bag is still in one of Monsieur K.'s desk drawers. I'm looking desperately for a mirror. That's always the way it is. My desires quickly become desperate. I need to see myself. The mirror has the effect of a memory. It retains my gestures and my expression. Seeing myself is remembering myself. Not forgetting myself. It is simultaneous remembering. The memory has a mirror effect. Moments are reflected, repeated. Misshapen, giant, or tiny moments. On the back of the mirror there is mercury. When you're there, on the other side of the mirror, at the source, at the roots of things and their images, there is poison you must swallow.

I hadn't gone so deep down inside myself, close to my cellars, close to my roots, for a long time. In our depths there are black wells, dungeons, dead ends. In our depths there is a haunted house, a desert land, a land between the tongues of the bay. Forgettable. Forgotten the day after tomorrow.

Steam is rising from an old coffee maker. Condensation covers the window. I feel like writing a name with my index finger. But no name comes to mind. It's been a long time since I haven't had a name to write on a steamed-up window. I see the curdled sky, the white turning in the white, becoming purple, the wind chasing the clouds and the sky advancing in wisps of smoke, retreating, advancing, and turning in circles.

I am already thinking of the jerky rhythm of the metro. I am thinking again of the jerky rhythm of this city. Its gaping mouth beckons me again. The descent into its labyrinth is the only life I know, the only dwelling I know.

It is time to go home.

Shumona Sinha was born and grew up in Calcutta, West Bengal. In 1990 she won Bengal's Best Young Poet award. She started learning French at the age of twenty-two and moved to Paris a few years later. Her first novel, *Fenêtre sur l'abîme*, was published in 2008. Her award-winning second novel, *Assommons les pauvres!*, was translated into German, Arabic, Italian and Hungarian, and adapted for the stage in Germany and Austria. Her third novel, *Calcutta* (2014), received the Prix du rayonnement de la langue et de la littérature françaises, awarded by the Académie française, and the Grand Prix du Roman of the Société des gens de lettres. Her most recent novel, *Le testament russe*, was published in March 2020 by Éditions Gallimard.

Teresa Lavender Fagan is a freelance translator from Chicago. She has translated over forty published works of non-fiction and fiction by authors ranging from Mircea Eliade, Hédi Kaddour and Vénus Khoury-Ghata (*The Last Days of Mandelstam* – shortlisted for the Oxford-Weidenfeld Prize) to the Nobel Laureate in Literature Jean-Marie Le Clézio.

AVAILABLE NOW FROM DEEP VELLUM

SHANE ANDERSON • *After the Oracle* • USA

MICHÈLE AUDIN • *One Hundred Twenty-One Days* • translated by Christiana Hills • FRANCE

BAE SUAH • *Recitation* • translated by Deborah Smith • SOUTH KOREA

MARIO BELLATIN • *Mrs. Murakami's Garden* • translated by Heather Cleary • *Beauty Salon* • translated by Shook • MEXICO

EDUARDO BERTI • *The Imagined Land* • translated by Charlotte Coombe • ARGENTINA

CARMEN BOULLOSA • *Texas: The Great Theft* • translated by Samantha Schnee • *Before* • translated by Peter Bush • *Heavens on Earth* • translated by Shelby Vincent • *The Book of Eve* • translated by Samantha Schnee • MEXICO

KB BROOKINS • *Freedom House* • USA

CHRISTINE BYL • *Lookout* • USA

CAYLIN CAPRA-THOMAS • *Iguana Iguana* • USA

MAGDA CÂRNECI • *FEM* • translated by Sean Cotter • ROMANIA

MIRCEA CĂRTĂRESCU • *Solenoid* • translated by Sean Cotter • ROMANIA

LEILA S. CHUDORI • *Home* • translated by John H. McGlynn • INDONESIA

JULIA CIMAFIEJEVA • *Motherfield* • translated by Valzhyna Mort & Hanif Abdurraqib • BELARUS

MATHILDE WALTER CLARK • *Lone Star* • translated by Martin Aitken & K. E. Semmel • DENMARK

PETER CONSTANTINE • *The Purchased Bride* • USA

TIM COURSEY • *Driving Lessons* • USA

LOGEN CURE • *Welcome to Midland: Poems* • USA

ANANDA DEVI • *Eve Out of Her Ruins* • translated by Jeffrey Zuckerman • *When the Night Agrees to Speak to Me* • translated by Kazim Ali • MAURITIUS

DHUMKETU • *The Shehnai Virtuoso* • translated by Jenny Bhatt • INDIA

PETER DIMOCK • *Daybook from Sheep Meadow* • USA

CLAUDIA ULLOA DONOSO • *Little Bird* • translated by Lily Meyer • PERU/NORWAY

LEYLÂ ERBIL • *A Strange Woman* • translated by Nermin Menemencioğlu & Amy Marie Spangler • TURKEY

RADNA FABIAS • *Habitus* • translated by David Colmer • CURAÇAO/NETHERLANDS

ROSS FARRAR • *Ross Sings Cheree & the Animated Dark: Poems* • USA

ALISA GANIEVA • *The Mountain and the Wall* • *Bride and Groom* • *Offended Sensibilities* • translated by Carol Apollonio • RUSSIA

FERNANDA GARCÍA LAO • *Out of the Cage* • translated by Will Vanderhyden • ARGENTINA

ANNE GARRÉTA • *Sphinx* • *Not One Day* • *In Concrete* • translated by Emma Ramadan • FRANCE

ALLA GORBUNOVA • *It's the End of the World, My Love* • translated by Elina Alter • RUSSIA

NIVEN GOVINDEN • *Diary of a Film* • GREAT BRITAIN

JÓN GNARR • *The Indian* • *The Pirate* • *The Outlaw* • translated by Lytton Smith • ICELAND

AVAILABLE NOW FROM DEEP VELLUM

GOETHE • *The Golden Goblet: Selected Poems* • *Faust, Part One* • translated by Zsuzsanna Ozsváth and Frederick Turner • GERMANY

SARA GOUDARZI • *The Almond in the Apricot* • USA

GISELA HEFFES • *Ischia* • translated by Grady C. Ray • ARGENTINA

NOEMI JAFFE • *What Are the Blind Men Dreaming?* • translated by Julia Sanches & Ellen Elias-Bursac • BRAZIL

PERGENTINO JOSÉ • *Red Ants* • MEXICO

TAISIA KITAISKAIA • *The Nightgown & Other Poems* • USA

SONG LIN • *The Gleaner Song: Selected Poems* • translated by Dong Li • CHINA

GYULA JENEI • *Always Different* • translated by Diana Senechal • HUNGARY

DIAA JUBAILI • *No Windmills in Basra* • translated by Chip Rossetti • IRAQ

JUNG YOUNG MOON • *Seven Samurai Swept Away in a River* • *Vaseline Buddha* • translated by Yewon Jung • SOUTH KOREA

ELENI KEFALA • *Time Stitches* • translated by Peter Constantine • CYPRUS

UZMA ASLAM KHAN • *The Miraculous True History of Nomi Ali* • PAKISTAN /USA

KIM YIDEUM • *Blood Sisters* • translated by Jiyoon Lee • SOUTH KOREA

JOSEFINE KLOUGART • *Of Darkness* • translated by Martin Aitken • DENMARK

ANDREY KURKOV • *Grey Bees* • *Diary of an Invasion* • translated by Boris Dralyuk • UKRAINE

YANICK LAHENS • *Moonbath* • translated by Emily Gogolak • *Sweet Undoings* • translated by Kaiama L. Glover • HAITI

JORGE ENRIQUE LAGE • *Freeway: La Movie* • translated by Lourdes Molina • CUBA

FOUAD LAROUI • *The Curious Case of Dassoukine's Trousers* • translated by Emma Ramadan • MOROCCO

MARIA GABRIELA LLANSOL • *The Geography of Rebels Trilogy: The Book of Communities; The Remaining Life; In the House of July & August* • translated by Audrey Young • PORTUGAL

TEDI LÓPEZ MILLS • *The Book of Explanations* • translated by Robin Myers • MEXICO

PABLO MARTÍN SÁNCHEZ • *The Anarchist Who Shared My Name* • translated by Jeff Diteman • SPAIN

DOROTA MASŁOWSKA • *Honey, I Killed the Cats* • translated by Benjamin Paloff • POLAND

BRICE MATTHIEUSSENT • *Revenge of the Translator* • translated by Emma Ramadan • FRANCE

ANTONIO MORESCO • *Clandestinity* • translated by Richard Dixon • ITALY

VALÉRIE MRÉJEN • *Black Forest* • translated by Katie Shireen Assef • FRANCE

STON MWANZA MUJILA • *Tram 83* • translated by Roland Glasser • *The River in the Belly: Poems* • translated by J. Bret Maney • DEMOCRATIC REPUBLIC OF CONGO

GORAN PETROVIĆ • *At the Lucky Hand, aka The Sixty-Nine Drawers* • translated by Peter Agnone • SERBIA

AVAILABLE NOW FROM DEEP VELLUM

LUDMILLA PETRUSHEVSKAYA • *The New Adventures of Helen: Magical Tales* • translated by Jane Bugaeva • *Kidnapped: A Story in Crimes* • translated by Marian Schwartz • RUSSIA

ILJA LEONARD PFEIJFFER • *La Superba* • translated by Michele Hutchison • NETHERLANDS

SERGIO PITOL • *The Art of Flight* • *The Journey* • *The Magician of Vienna* • *Mephisto's Waltz: Selected Short Stories* • *The Love Parade* • translated by George Henson • MEXICO

JULIE POOLE • *Bright Specimen* • USA

N. PRABHAKARAN • *Diary of a Malayali Madman* • translated by Jayasree Kalathil • INDIA

EDUARDO RABASA • *A Zero-Sum Game* • translated by Christina MacSweeney • MEXICO

ZAHIA RAHMANI • *"Muslim": A Novel* • translated by Matt Reeck • FRANCE/ALGERIA

MANON STEFFAN ROS • *The Blue Book of Nebo* • WALES

JUAN RULFO • *The Golden Cockerel & Other Writings* • translated by Douglas J. Weatherford • MEXICO

IGNACIO RUIZ-PÉREZ • *Isles of Firm Ground* • translated by Mike Soto • MEXICO

ETHAN RUTHERFORD • *Farthest South & Other Stories* • USA

TATIANA RYCKMAN • *The Ancestry of Objects* • USA

JIM SCHUTZE • *The Accommodation* • USA

JANE SAGINAW • *Because the World Is Round* • USA

OLEG SENTSOV • *Life Went On Anyway* • translated by Uilleam Blacker • UKRAINE

MIKHAIL SHISHKIN • *Calligraphy Lesson: The Collected Stories* • translated by Marian Schwartz, Leo Shtutin, Mariya Bashkatova, Sylvia Maizell • RUSSIA

ÓFEIGUR SIGURÐSSON • *Öræfi: The Wasteland* • translated by Lytton Smith • ICELAND

NOAH SIMBLIST, ed. • *Tania Bruguera: The Francis Effect* • CUBA

DANIEL SIMON, ed. • *Dispatches from the Republic of Letters* • USA

SHUMONA SINHA • *Down with the Poor!* • translated by Teresa Fagan • INDIA/FRANCE

MUSTAFA STITOU • *Two Half Faces* • translated by David Colmer • NETHERLANDS

SOPHIA TERAZAWA • *Winter Phoenix: Testimonies in Verse* • Anon • USA

MÄRTA TIKKANEN • *The Love Story of the Century* • translated by Stina Katchadourian • SWEDEN

KRISTÍN SVAVA TÓMASDÓTTIR • *Herostories* • translated by K. B. Thors • ICELAND

ROBERT TRAMMELL • *Jack Ruby & the Origins of the Avant-Garde in Dallas & Other Stories* • USA

YANA VAGNER • *To the Lake* • translated by Maria Wiltshire • RUSSIA

BENJAMIN VILLEGAS • *ELPASO: A Punk Story* • translated by Jay Noden • SPAIN

S. YARBERRY • *A Boy in the City* • USA

SYLVIA AGUILAR ZÉLENY • *Trash* • translated by JD Pluecker • MEXICO

SERHIY ZHADAN • *Voroshilovgrad* • translated by Reilly Costigan-Humes & Isaac Wheeler • UKRAINE